D0040636

Scranton, Pennsylvania

LIES AND SHADOWS

Pam Hart

A KISMET® Romance

METEOR PUBLISHING CORPORATION

Bensalem, Pennsylvania

Special thanks to Mike Gibbons of Gibbons Bail Bonds in Council Bluffs, Iowa, for sparking the idea for this story.

And thanks to my brother, Jim, in McCook, Nebraska, for letting me borrow the real Molly. What a dog!

To everyone who believed I could do it, even when I didn't. My heartfelt thanks.

PAM HART

Jack of all trades, master of none, Pam has been a high school teacher, probation officer, social service worker, secretary, and a manucurist. She lives in Omaha with her three children, one cat, and their most recent addition, a gerbil. Teaching Criminal Justice at a local community college provides a never-ending supply of information for her writing.

PROLOGUE

The shrill ring of a telephone rent the predawn silence. A large hand shot out, fumbled once, and yanked the receiver off its cradle. Swearing under his breath, Gabe jerked it to his ear. "Yeah?"

The line snapped and popped as though from far away. "Hey, Sanders!" the voice clipped out. "You there?"

Rolling onto his back, Gabe scratched his chest through a bramble of dark hair, and absently groped toward the nightstand for his cigarettes. "Who wants to know?"

"Parrish."

The name echoed in the black night and brought a flood of memories. Dark memories of a black time. Fuzzy memories from the bottom of a whiskey bottle. If not for Rick Parrish, Gabe would still be in hell, viewing the world through bloodshot eyes and an anesthetized haze.

"Hey, buddy—" The phone line crackled, or was it a garbled laugh on the other end? "You still there?"

7

"Yeah . . ."

"Look," Rick began, "I need you to run an errand."

"I don't do that stuff anymore." Gabe lit a cigarette and drew in a long drag before sending the round of smoke skyward. "I assign it to somebody else."

"Gotta be you. Bruce Hunter's slipperier than river-bottom mud. The French want him, Interpol wants him, and I want him. I want him real bad."

Gabe digested the last bit of information and squinted through the swirling smoke. "Why?"

"He's been running industrial espionage through France and finally stepped on all the wrong toes. I want him for more personal reasons. Had him cornered at the Swiss border, and the bastard gave me the slip. Made me look like an idiot. He's coming your way. Nail him and hand him over, okay?"

No, Gabe wanted to say, *it wasn't okay,* but what the hell could he do? He owed Parrish. Owed him big.

Screw France and screw Interpol, Gabe thought. For anyone else, he'd reassign the case—period! The end. These days he only got involved when an underling couldn't handle it. This Hunter character sounded like a world-class wuss. It wouldn't take much to handle him. Besides, delegating authority was an executive perk.

But this was Rick. Gabe couldn't refuse. He grabbed an ashtray and settled back into three king-sized pillows. "Who you working for these days?"

"Interpol mostly. I'm tied up with another case, or I'd hop over and lend you a hand." A heavy pause fed through the line. "You still a card-carrying bounty hunter?"

Gabe's teeth parted in a predatory grin. "You bet."

"Good. There's a high-loaded bounty on this dude."

"Enough to retire on Bimini?"

"Hell, you'll be able to *buy* Bimini. I'm faxing paperwork and reports right now. You'll have Interpol's authority, so check with the local cops if you need something legal. Anything else is up to you."

The overseas connection sparked and spit. Gabe thought the line had died until Rick's voice floated back.

"One other thing, Sanders. He's headed for his sister's, a woman named Devereaux." Rick hesitated.

Instinct said there was more, and Gabe wasn't going to like it. "What else?"

"She's got kids."

"I'd rather French-kiss a rattler than work with kids." Gabe ground his cigarette in the ashtray. "How many?"

"Three."

"Ah, hell," Gabe groaned, his head cracking against the oak headboard. If he had any sense, he'd tell Parrish to shove off. But he couldn't. Erasing this debt would leave him totally free, owing nothing to another living soul. He liked the idea too much to let it go.

"Sorry, buddy," Rick said. "If there was any other way, I'd have grabbed it." Tension pulsed through the line. "Get Hunter, Gabe. Do it any way you can, but get him."

A doleful sigh rushed through his lips, and Gabe slid the receiver back on its cradle. He lit another cigarette and drew a long, slow lungful. What the hell had he done to deserve this? How had he tempted Fate, that faithless bitch? Six years he'd avoided life, worked the shadows, stayed alone and uninvolved except for a few flings with women who knew the score. How the devil had this come down?

He shoved back the sheet and yanked on his Levi's. Without bothering to zip or snap them, he stalked downstairs to the fax machine in his office. It purred and beeped, signaling Interpol's transmission.

Glancing at the first page, Gabe noted the Devereauxs lived in Ponca Hills, a loose collection of sprawling acreages north of Omaha. He nodded and lit another cigarette. Nice area. Real nice. They must be pretty well off.

The mother was one *Victoria Alexis,* age thirty-five, five foot ten, one hundred thirty pounds. A quick flash of long legs, the curve of a sleek calf, streaked through his mind. A slow whistle eased through his teeth. Modern technology sure painted a shapely image.

Page two spit out Mrs. Devereaux's pertinent information. College drop out, wife, mother, current widow, recently moved from Canada. Blah, blah, blah. Where were the dirty details? No one was this squeaky clean. Not in this day and age.

Maybe the world isn't all garbage, Sanders.

Gabe snorted. Yeah, right, and he was Henry the Eighth.

Page three shook in his hand. Twelve-year-old-Jillian, nine-year-old Michael, and six-year-old Anastasia. Damn!

Gabe fell into a wing-back chair. Victoria Devereaux's youngest child was the same age his daughter would have been. That is, if she'd lived longer than a lousy eight weeks.

Overwhelming pain gnawed at the empty pocket where his heart should be. He squeezed his burning eyes shut, forced back the image of a tiny body in a small white coffin.

In a blaze of anger, he damned Rick for dredging it

all up again. Gabe damned himself for owing the favor, and damned the past. Nothing good ever came from emotion. Nothing.

He snatched up the next page and read on. *Bruce Hunter*. In the limelight, an exclusive, internationally recognized photographer. In reality, a courier of industrial espionage. Interpol had had its eye on him for the past three years. His visits to his sister might appear random to outsiders, but according to Interpol, they coincided with known drops outside Continental Europe. He arrived supposedly to see his nieces and nephew, and wind down from a hectic career. A dual career.

A user, Gabe sneered with silent disdain. Only a scumbag involved hapless bystanders to cover up a scheme.

Had he dragged his sister into his inventive web? Hunter stayed with her, lying low until the heat cooled. Was Victoria a willing, unwilling, or innocent party? Gabe almost laughed. There were no innocents. Not in the shadows.

One way or another, he'd crack this thing wide open. If he was lucky, something would break in a day or two. If not, he'd make his own breaks.

An addendum rolled out of the fax machine. Reading the update drained the tension from Gabe's shoulders. Seemed that Mrs. Victoria Devereaux had recently been hired as a medical sales representative. Since the job required travel, she'd placed an ad in Sunday's *World-Herald* for a nanny. A local service was handling the resumes, but Mrs. Devereaux was handling the interviews.

With his contacts, the job was Gabe's for the taking. It was easy, too easy. Like taking a pacifier from a newborn. There was only one catch. "Twenty-four hours a day with a bunch of yard apes."

He raked a disgusted hand through his hair and glared into the gloom. Hell, if worse came to worst, he'd ship them off to summer camp!

ONE

Exasperated, Victoria tore her attention from her oldest, and strongest-willed, child. Too many times these past years she felt as if she'd run a mental footrace with Jillian—and wasn't always sure who'd won. Westminster chimes pealed through her home once again. She glared at the door. She didn't care to deal with anything or anyone else this afternoon. Whoever it was would have to leave.

Muttering a word her children didn't know she knew, she grasped the doorknob as the impatient caller rang yet again. Unable to keep the mounting irritation at bay, she jerked the door open. "Yes? What is it?"

A tall, formidable male body unfolded from the wrought-iron railing in the shadow of her porch. Thick, tobacco brown hair was sleeked back in a queue. Mirrored sunglasses masked his eyes in emotionless, glassy pools that cast an unnerving reflection of her own frown. Her breath whooshed out.

A teal polo shirt melted across his broad shoulders and down his solid chest before tucking into well-faded,

13

low-slung jeans. The denim, having seen better days, sported a long, horizontal rip in the left knee. The beginnings of a well-honed thigh peppered with dark brown hair peeked brazenly through.

He stepped forward. She took an involuntary step back. His size—a quick estimation said about six foot one—wasn't overpowering. His total appearance was. He was dark and masculine; every pore radiated M-A-L-E, every cell spelled S-E-X-Y.

Her breathing slowed; her heart thudded a heavy cadence against her ribs. Without conscious permission, her body kindled in a primordial female response. She took a protective step back.

"Ms. Devereaux," he said, the corners of his mouth quirking just the slightest, as though he knew how he'd made her feel. "I'm here for the job."

His voice, a quiet, mellow baritone, wrapped around her like thick, pure honey, nestling her in its warmth and perfection. A lovely voice, to be sure, she decided and—

"Ms. Devereaux? You okay?"

Off balance for a moment, she shook herself. "Oh, sorry. Outwitting my oldest daughter muddles my mind, Mr. . . . ?"

"Sanders, Gabriel Sanders." He hesitated, glancing down for a moment. "About the job," he said, pulling several sheets of paper from a back pocket.

"Job?" The man certainly dressed strangely for an interview. Or maybe she was losing the few marbles she had left. "I'm sorry again, Mr. Sanders—"

"Gabe," he supplied smoothly.

"Mr. Sanders," she said. "What job?"

"Your advertisement. The Nanny Service sent me."

This man? This overpowering, virile specimen of the

male gender wanted to be a nanny? Her nanny! Her head spun, and she grabbed the door for support.

"Ms. Devereaux," came his melodious voice, "are you sure you're okay?" Strong fingers gripped her shoulders and ushered her inside. Before she could catch her breath, he closed the door behind them.

"Now, see here," she began, quickly recovering herself. "I did not invite you in."

"No, you didn't," he said, lounging insolently against the door. "But I did expect an interview out of the deal."

He peeled off the aviator shades, and she found herself staring into thickly lashed hazel eyes, beautiful, sharp, and intelligent. If the glasses had mirrored her, those greenish gold orbs mirrored this man's soul. Victoria imagined she read cunning, sincerity, and numbed pain in their depths.

He might be an athlete, a beefcake model, or a rebel without a cause, but a nanny? "What do you want from me?"

His lips parted to answer; his gaze drilled into hers. A leisurely pause flared between them, lending a sensual spin to his words. "The job, of course."

Pleasure sifted through Victoria, settling low in her chest before she could check it. "I don't think so," she said with a shake of her head.

"I mean," she said more forcefully, trying to back off in a graceful but firm manner, "you're not quite what I had in mind for the position."

He smiled. Disarmingly. Meltingly. Like Michael caught in mischief. Wanting to smile back, she steeled herself against the unbidden response. He was a grown man, not a mischievous boy.

"One measly interview?" he coaxed, still grinning

like a reprobate. "Maybe I could change your mind about—" he let the word hang in the air "—things."

"I really don't think—"

"Am I too old?" he rushed on. "I'm only thirty-eight. I think I have a few good years left," he said with another breath-catching grin.

"No, you're not too old." She hated the softening in her heart, but she could never refuse a scamp, especially one with the smile of an angel.

"Are you a chauvinist, Mrs. Devereaux?" He crossed his arms over his broad, solid-looking chest. "You think a man can't be as good a nanny as a woman?"

"No," she hastened to assure him. "It isn't that."

"Then what is? Have you hired someone else?"

"Not yet. All my candidates got positions elsewhere."

"I could start immediately," he pressed. "I'm between jobs at the moment."

Like a woman going under for the third time, Victoria sighed in polite resignation and turned toward her office. "Very well, then. Follow me."

So this was Victoria Devereaux, Gabe thought. Live and in the flesh. Well, as close to in the flesh as he'd ever get. The fax hadn't begun to do her justice. This little lady—and she certainly was a lady, every damned inch of·her—was a surprise. Now that he was up close and personal, he found it hard to believe she was part of her brother's setup. But lots of smooth feminine packages were black widows in disguise. This one was a definite puzzlement.

She radiated culture and refinement from the top of her coal black upsweep to that little wiggle in her fanny he'd bet she didn't know she had. Just the kiss of a British accent gave her the firepower of simultaneous H-bombs. A grin sneaked out despite his best efforts.

"Something amuses you, Mr. Sanders?"

"No . . . not at all. You were saying?"

She drew herself up ramrod-straight behind her desk. Gabe could almost hear her foot tapping in irritation. Maybe his smile needed more work.

"I said your resume seems to be in order." A gentle lift of her dynamite pink lips arrowed straight to his gut. "I see you've recently moved back to Omaha."

He nodded agreement, but the lie tweaked his conscience. Fine time for ethics, Sanders.

"So have we, from Toronto. I'm afraid my oldest hasn't taken too kindly to it, however. Do you have much experience with obstinate teenagers?" She raised inquisitive brows.

"Uh . . . every home has one," he returned, trying, for some odd reason, to avoid a direct lie. "I consider them a personal challenge."

She stared at him a long moment, and he could almost see the calculations whirling in her head. His answer must have convinced her, and she glanced back at his resume.

"I'm really looking for less than a nanny but more than a baby-sitter. When I'm home and around the children, I'll take over," she said. "Light housekeeping also required."

"No problem," he said easily. How difficult could housekeeping be?

She shot him an assessing, pointed look. "I see you've been a nanny—"

"Household helper," he supplied.

"Household helper . . ." A touch of aggravation threaded her words.

He'd broken through her refined exterior, Gabe thought, if only for a brief moment. Chalk one up for him.

". . . for only five years?"

"Four," he supplied smoothly, varnishing over the truth. Investigative cohorts had his references staged and primed for any check-up calls. His resume and background were airtight, and best of all, his cohorts had been busy hiring other applicants away. He didn't even have to wait for Victoria to take the bait. Hell, he was a shoo-in.

"Before that, you were a juvenile probation officer. Why the switch?"

"Burnout." He lightly shrugged off the latest lie. "Clichéd, but true. I thought I could change the world." And there was the god's truth. "I find it easier to stop kid problems where they start. In the home."

She nodded her understanding and rose to end the meeting. "Well, everything certainly looks in order—" She broke off, frowning at the partially closed door.

He followed her gaze. A large Golden Lab nosed the door wider and sauntered in.

"Molly," Victoria said, "go to your rug."

Instead of obeying, the beast came and sat by Gabe. They exchanged a mutually suspicious look. Gabe mentally weighed the dog in at about seventy-five pounds of solid muscle from chest to tail. He didn't care to dwell on the animal's long, strong teeth; her jaw could crush an arm.

"Molly," Victoria ordered. "Your rug . . . now!"

Gabe hoped the animal couldn't read character; after all, he'd calmly lied through his teeth to its owner.

"I'm sorry," Victoria said, standing behind her well-polished desk. "She usually minds very well."

Molly's solid tail thump-thump-thumped against Gabe's Reeboks. Well-trained, maybe. Obstinate, definitely.

He hid his grin behind a hand. The animal dipped her head and inched forward. Her big amber eyes gazed soulfully up. Before Gabe could blink, Molly nestled her chin on his thigh, giving him her silent blessing. The family pet liked him, and he was safe from bodily harm. Man's best friend.

"Good grief," Victoria said, exasperation lacing her words. "I think she's dotty for you."

Gabe had to agree. The Lab looked at him in a way he could only describe as "lovesick." He could hardly disengage his leg from the mutt when she cast moon eyes at him.

"Molly Ann, there you are." A dark-haired moppet planted hands on her tiny hips. Anastasia.

"Shame on you," she scolded her pet. "You know you're not s'posed to be in here." She turned an angelic face to her mother. "Sorry, Mama."

The ghost of a smile tickled Victoria's mouth before she nodded. The child walked up to Gabe, watching him closely with guileless gray eyes. He could see the wheels turning in her mind, evaluating him. "Who're you?" she asked.

Watching this child, a living example of his shattered dreams, affected him like an upper cut to the solar plexus. His breath hissed out. "Gabe," he said, realizing he'd been staring, and silent too long. "Gabe Sanders."

"Darling, take Molly and run along," Victoria said. "Mr. Sanders and I have business to discuss."

The child turned obediently, but hesitated. Resting her elbows on the arm of Gabe's chair, she leaned toward him as if imparting great wisdom. "We don't really need a nanny," she said earnestly, and dropped her voice to a stage whisper. "I'm afraid Mamma's gonna take the lady with the twitchy lips."

Gabe sat rooted to the chair, transfixed by her every movement. The child was true innocence. For a moment he thought he'd drown in the fathomless depths of her eyes.

She considered him a moment longer, nodded sagely, and turned to her dog. "C'mon, Molly. Let's have tea."

The animal lifted its head, gazing from her mistress back to Gabe. "Go on," he prompted.

Molly stood and ambled toward the door, turning back to Gabe one last time. "Move it," he said, not really knowing what to say to an overardent animal.

"Thank you," Victoria said as Molly's long, blond tail disappeared out the door. "As I was saying, everything in your resume seems in order, Mr. Sanders. I'll check your references and call you if I'm interested."

Which she wasn't, Gabe thought as she ushered him very graciously out the door he'd worked so hard to get through. He'd only gotten this far because he'd backed her into a corner, and she was too polite to throw him out on his can.

He'd done his best to goad her—the clothes, the sunglasses, the attitude—to test her and see if she was what the report had stated: old-fashioned and well bred.

She was. He looked forward to scratching the surface, digging a little deeper and seeing what else he could find. Did her polish go clear to the bone, or was it merely skin-deep veneer covering another black widow?

"Oh, Mother! He was wonderful. You hired him, didn't you?" Jillian blurted out at supper.

"No, I did not," Victoria said, knowing exactly who *he* was. Somehow he'd managed to put their usually suspicious watchdog under his spell. Good thing Victoria was more discerning. "We don't know him. I have to check references."

"Who cares? All we've seen in Nebraska is corn and cows. The only people you interview are old fogies who dress like church ladies. This guy is hot. Totally awesome to the max!"

Victoria speared her daughter with her sternest, most disapproving glare. Michael twittered and received the same.

"Aw, Mum," he said, shrugging a small shoulder, "a guy could help me with soccer and stuff."

"I know, darling." Victoria resumed eating, but tasted nothing. Gabriel Sanders wouldn't be hired. He was too confident, too male, too . . . hot.

"Mama?" a small voice piped from the end of the table. "Me 'n Molly like him," Anastasia said with great finality.

"Molly and I, dear."

"Yeah, 'n his lips don't twitch."

Too true. Chiseled to perfection, they matched his rough-hewn, masculine features quite well. But her decision stuck. She had to protect her children. "Lips don't make a nanny."

"Ah, phooey," Anastasia said.

Victoria wasn't certain, but she thought Molly growled.

TWO

No way was she hiring Gabriel Sanders! Victoria fumed and stalked across the parking lot to the nursing home. Copies of several resumés sprouted from her open shoulder bag and scraped against her periwinkle linen slacks.

His references had checked out, not that she'd thought otherwise. Everyone she'd spoken to, including The Nanny Service, gave him glowing reports.

On the outside, on paper, he was everything she could want—in a nanny, she hastened to add. But on the inside? A quick memory flashed.

His languid stance, the length and breadth of his frame, intense and intelligent eyes. She shivered. Whatever was on the inside was best left there.

She'd come too far and worked too hard to get tripped up by a broad set of shoulders. She wasn't buying into that old, tired game again.

Victoria marched through streakless glass doors. There was no time to dwell on her nanny—or lack of one. Her heels clicked against the well-polished floor and echoed down the long hall. Steps slowing, she gathered her strength.

Usually when she visited her mother, unseeing eyes and blank stares of confusion met her. On occasion, her mother was competent and rational, remembering Victoria with love and affection. Even rarer times, she was met by a surly stranger.

Like last week. Victoria had entered the room, a bouquet of fresh-cut daisies in one hand, Anastasia in the other. A nurse hovered over her mother, speaking in a soft, soothing voice. Not a good sign.

Her mother'd taken one vacant look and frowned. "Oh, rats," she'd said, "the bitch is back."

It was Alzheimer's, a senseless, disorienting disease, speaking for the mother she loved, but the knowledge didn't lessen the hurt, or ease Victoria's mind. Now, standing outside the wooden door marked 306 HUNTER, ROSE, Victoria squared her shoulders and entered the room.

An embroidered shawl rested around her mother's frail shoulders. Rose looked up, a smile of recognition lighting her face and her eyes. "Victoria! My dear, how nice to see you," she said, raising her cheek for a kiss.

Once again love and acceptance rested in the soft blue eyes. Victoria's pent-up breath rushed out, and she blinked back sudden tears. She would hold this visit in her heart, cherish it as a talisman.

Rose patted a chair next to her. "How's the university?"

A deep, profound sadness swirled through Victoria. Her mother was coherent, at least about the past. It would do no good to bring it to her attention. Any explanations only frightened and upset her mother. Today she knew her daughter, and that was enough. "I'm fine, Mother. How are you?"

Rose smiled. "I'm crocheting a hat and muffler for Bruce," she said, reaching into an overstuffed bag of yarn at her feet. "You know how cold it gets at Michigan State. I hope he comes home for Christmas this year. . . ."

Victoria nodded, half listening to the wandering thoughts. Although she and Bruce finished college years ago, her brother never made it home for traditional family holidays. He managed to pop in just often enough to soothe ruffled feathers, but it wasn't enough. Victoria could use his advice and strong shoulder to lean on. Especially now, when her mother's health demanded attention, Victoria needed his support. Little was forthcoming.

". . . such a nice young man," Rose was saying.

"I'm sorry, Mother. What did you say?"

"Well, this, dear." Rose grabbed the resumés and waved them under her daughter's nose. "Maxine's boy."

"Boy?" Victoria frowned, trying to regain the gist of the conversation.

"Maxine Sanders. We work nights at the hospital." Her mother's brows furrowed together. "Your memory seems to be fading, dear. Are you feeling all right?"

No, she was light-headed, off kilter. Sanders? Maxine's boy? How could that be?

"Maxine's husband died ten years ago, and she's raised three boys by herself. Gabriel's quite the young man. Helped support the family with his own lawn business when he was sixteen. Works two jobs and manages to attend college, too. Such a nice family," she said. "And Sally Case? My former supervisor? Well, it seems . . ."

Victoria tuned her mother's rambling words out with

practiced ease. Her mother had worked with his? Impossible. Victoria would've remembered the name.

But in her early twenties, Victoria hadn't understood the beginnings of Alzheimer's: meandering thoughts, forgetfulness, increasing bouts of confusion. If her mother had mentioned Maxine, Gabriel, or any other Sanders, Victoria wouldn't have paid the announcement much attention.

Drat the man! Not only did he hold her dog's affection, her children's admiration, and the high esteem of his past employers, her mother had granted a benediction of her own.

So what's the problem?

Plenty. Before she knew it, the children would like him, respect him, and finally come to lean on him. And of course, when they needed him most, he'd be gone. The emotional fallout would be devastating.

No other reason?

Victoria hesitated. Visions of thick, tobacco brown hair in a sexy queue, sensuous lips almost quirking at the corners in a semismile, and strong, warm hands cupping her shoulders jammed her maternal radar before she shook herself clear.

No way. He wouldn't do, and that was that.

Gray thunderheads boiled in the northern sky. The atmosphere armed itself for a bruiser of a storm. Helluva night for it, too, Gabe thought, lighting a cigarette.

He glared at the churning charcoal clouds, feeling as dark and ready to rumble as they looked. A twenty-four-hour bender and a two-fisted fight could do him a world of good. The waiting was killing him. Four days had come and gone. Still no word from Victoria Devereaux. What the hell was she waiting for? Mary Poppins?

He was four days closer to Hunter's ETA. Four days late on setting up the scam.

Kids or no kids, the easiest place to bust Uncle Bruce was in his sister's home. Easier, quicker, and less messy.

Pacing his darkened living room, Gabe barely noticed when the storm hit. Howling wind swirled around the house. Heavy rains beat down with a fury Gabe understood. Arms folded across his chest, he stared out the picture window. Lightning sliced and slashed through the black night.

He inhaled deeply on his cigarette and blew smoke rings in the air, envying Mother Nature her violent outburst. He had to get in that house soon. Everything else was secondary.

Once inside, he'd have to deal with Victoria, but how? Her soft curves and inherent femininity fanned emotions as charged and explosive as the storm outside. Too bad he couldn't deal with her the way he'd like. One on one. Straight on and straight forward. Man to woman.

God, he thought, stubbing his cigarette out with unnecessary force. Could he live under the same roof without touching her, wanting her, possessing her? Dammit! He didn't know. Hopefully the kids would hate him, or the dog would bite him. Anything except Victoria getting under his skin.

A brilliant sunrise winked over the bluffs. The storm had washed away a layer of summer dust, and with it any lingering doubts. Gabe raked his fingers through his newly shortened hair. Thinking maybe he'd scared her off on his first interview, he completely revamped his image. One last check of the crease in his chino slacks and he knocked on the solid oak door.

"Yes, Mr. Sanders?" Wedged between the door and the frame, Victoria shielded the family's inner sanctum with her body. And a damn fine one at that, Gabe noted. Her voice was a little huskier than he remembered, a little breathier. "What can I do for you?" she asked.

Oh, sister. Don't ask. "The job? Remember?"

"Oh. Yes. Well. I haven't decided yet."

What was to decide? She didn't have an available candidate, so why the hesitation, unless . . . She didn't *want* to hire him. *She* didn't want to hire *him*? "You don't want to hire me."

Victoria shifted her gaze to a nebulous area behind his left shoulder. "No . . . that is . . . your resumé was very nice."

Gabe almost smiled. She didn't have the barracuda instinct to tell him, "No dice, slick" or "Go straight to hell." No, she danced around with thank yous and I'm sorrys.

"Can we talk about this? One on one," he said. This time he smiled, and her gaze flew from whatever she found so fascinating behind him to his face.

"I don't—"

"You don't grant the man you're kissing off the pleasure of a face-to-face encounter?" he dared, silently hoping she couldn't refuse.

She stiffened and rose to the bait. "I'm not kissing you off."

"You're not hiring me, either." He opened the door wider and leaned forward. She looked pale and wan, as if she'd spent a sleepless night. He wondered if anyone had spent it with her and, unaccountably irritated, tossed the thought aside. If she was tired and more vulnerable, it was to his advantage. This was the time to apply pressure. A much-needed point for his side.

Another stroke of long-ignored ethics twinged inside, rousing a deeply buried instinct. Gabe quickly doused it. Time was running out, and with it, his options.

She stepped onto the large, shaded porch. "All right, Mr. Sanders. What is it you want?"

Her voice affected a man like fine champagne, going straight to the head. She could lead a lesser man a merry chase, drive him dizzy with desire.

The Interpol report on her had intrigued him. A bona fide lady sounded too good to be true. At the interview, he'd wanted the woman in her to recognize the man in him.

Maybe he'd come on too strong and scared her off. Maybe that's why she hadn't hired him, why she was backing away from him right now. "You know," he said, unable to keep the laughter out of his voice, "if you back up much farther, you'll fall off the porch. I'm not Attila the Hun."

"I know that." She smoothed invisible lines off her royal blue walking shorts. "And I'm not backing up."

"Yes, you are. Do I scare you?"

Her head snapped up. Her eyes sparkled silver with irritation. "Certainly not."

"Glad to hear it," he confessed—truthfully for once. "Every time I'm around you, you look like a doe caught in oncoming headlights. I can understand your reluctance to hire a man for this position, but, Mrs. Devereaux, I swear on my mother's grave, I'm not a pedophile, a serial killer, or an axe murderer. I just want to be your nanny."

"Your mother's grave?" Her wide eyes filled with compassion and sorrow. "I didn't know. I'm so sorry."

Confused, Gabe shook his head. "There wasn't any way you could've known. It was a long time ago."

Victoria leaned a shoulder against the house. Echoes

of childish laughter and splashing echoed from the backyard. "You're not going to believe this," she said with a dynamite smile that kicked him in the gut. She shook her head, loosening humidity curls he longed to smooth back.

Steeling himself against the urge, he slid his hands into his back pockets. Her gaze slid to his waist. Heat flashed thorough Gabe like last night's lightning. "Believe what?"

Her gaze flew to his face, searching, evaluating. He hoped he made the grade.

"Our mothers knew one another," she said. "They worked together at Jennie Edmundsen Hospital years ago."

Gabe stopped short. "What?"

Victoria shrugged a delicate shoulder. "I hardly believed it myself. When I visited my mother yesterday, she remembered your mother—Maxine?" At his nod, she continued. "Weird, huh?"

"More than weird," he agreed. "I don't remember her mentioning any . . ."

"Hunter," she supplied. "Her name is Rose Hunter."

Recognition dawned, and Gabe lifted his brows. "The one that sneaked in a game of five-card stud on the night shift?"

Victoria chuckled. "Yes. Small world, isn't it?"

She didn't know the half of it, Gabe mused. "Mom said Rose was a real card shark. Always remembered every card played," he said with a fond smile. "How is she?"

Victoria's shoulders drooped, her mouth thinned, and a sigh heavier than she had a right to possess slipped through extraordinarily kissable lips. "She's in a nursing home," she said. "Her heart is extremely weak, but

. . .'' She drew in a deep shudder. ''The Alzheimer's is so hard to cope with.''

''Alzheimer's? Your mother?''

Victoria stared off in the distance at the rolling hillside, and nodded.

''Jeez, Victoria,'' he said, slipping into the use of her first name with no problem. ''I'm sorry.''

''That's the way it goes,'' she said softly. ''We all have burdens to bear.''

Damn, what lousy timing. Gabe would've liked nothing more than to soothe the weariness off her face, massage those dainty shoulders until whatever invisible load she carried faded into the background. He wouldn't mind a heavy round of hot sex, for that matter, but he knew the rules. She was a forever-after type of woman, and he was a fly-by-night kind of guy with nothing to offer. Still, she got to him on a me-Tarzan-you-Jane level, but that couldn't stop him. ''How did my name come up in conversation with your mother?''

''She saw your resumé in my purse. Sometimes she tends to ramble, and before I could blink, she'd given me the lowdown.''

''She's coherent?''

Victoria eyed him, assessing and evaluating him again. ''Today she was,'' she said at last. ''But her mind was about fifteen years in the past.''

He heard the anguish in her voice, and fought an unfamiliar bout of sympathy. ''Hire me.''

A strangled sound came from Victoria, and she spun around. ''No.''

Fists planted on his hips, he frowned at her. ''Give me ten reasons why not.''

Oh, brother, Victoria thought. Where did she start? He was definitely a go-getter, came from a good family with midwestern values, seemed competent, efficient, and well mannered—albeit a bit pushy. But he also had the smile of a scamp, the voice of an angel, and a mouth-watering build. He was too attractive on all levels. A female nanny would be like a roommate in the house. But Gabriel Sanders as a roommate? It defied rational thought.

"Can't do it, can you?" Gabriel sauntered over to her with a long-legged, hip-rolling gait. "Come on," he coaxed with whiskey-smoothness. "I'm here. I'm ready, willing, and—" he paused, leaning toward her with infuriating confidence and innuendo "—certainly more than able."

He snapped back. "Besides, your mother likes me."

What conceit! What chutzpah! What gall to make such an assumption! Damn, now he had her swearing, even if the oaths were unspoken.

"Well, didn't she?"

"Yes," Victoria hissed.

"Then what's our problem? I'm here, so why not take advantage of it?"

"Because I don't want you to take advantage of us."

He pressed a large palm against his chest. *"Moi?"*

She bit back her smile. A devil with an angel's name. Why'd he have to go and show her a softer, humorous side?

"Come on, Victoria," Gabe said, striving for his smoothest, most persuasive voice. She was weakening. Any minute she'd cave in. "What have you got to lose?"

The minute he asked the question, he could've bit his lip off. The open emotions scampering across her elegant face told him she had much to lose. So did her children. And, Gabe feared, so did he.

Victoria straightened her shoulders as though marshaling strength for another round. "Why do you want this so bad?"

Gazing into her eyes, Gabe paused. He'd bailed the

scum of the earth out of jail for more than six years, engaged in high-speed chases, occasional shoot-outs, and beat the ever-lovin' hell out of bail jumpers when necessary. He'd stared down the best of the worst, lied through his teeth to mothers, wives, and girlfriends to get what he needed when he needed it, but God help him, he couldn't lie to Victoria again.

"When I first dropped by," he began, rubbing his hand across his forehead, "I just wanted the job." He drew a deep breath. "But meeting Anastasia . . . I can't really explain it."

"Your usual eloquence is failing you, Mr. Sanders."

"And you've got a helluva sharp tongue, Mrs. Devereaux. I can think of a lot better uses for it than flaying my hide."

He stepped toward her. She stepped back. Once. Twice.

His eyes widened, and his arm shot out. "Wait—"

Victoria leaned away and toppled off the edge of the wooden porch, landing on the cement scalloping around the flower bed. Her ankle twisted, and pain shot up her right leg. "O-o-h!" Victoria groaned. "My God."

Gabe bounded off the porch in a lithe catapult and lit beside her. "Victoria," he muttered. "I warned you—"

"Oh, shut up," she moaned.

Gabe glared at her, but clamped his jaw together. "I heard a pop. You might've broken something. Hold still."

She raised up on one elbow, wincing and brushing dirt and twigs off her disheveled clothes. "I'm fine."

"We'll see," he muttered, and pulled out a snow white handkerchief. He pressed it against her hairline over a small, oozing scrape. "Hold this. You've got a contusion."

"Contusion?" she mocked, but followed directions.

"A nasty boo-boo," he supplied with a wicked grin.

"Thank you, Dr. Sanders."

"Well," he persisted, despite the pain etched in her eyes and bracketing her mouth, "at least your kids will have dynamite first aid in any emergency."

"Don't you ever give up?"

"Never," he growled. "I always get my man—er, woman . . . kids. Whatever," he muttered, kicking his mental backside and hoping she wouldn't notice the slip of words.

What Victoria noticed was his hand perched on her right knee. Pushing him away, she tried to move her leg. Her half moan didn't break the surface. She valiantly bit her lip.

"Okay, tough cookie," he said, sliding his hand down her shin. "Let Papa see the problem."

She tried to pull away. "Don't patronize me, Sanders."

"Fair enough," Gabe said, gently probing along her shin and calf. "But don't patronize me, either, Mrs. Devereaux. You're in a bad way here, both physically and family-wise. If my suspicions are right, you're going to be off that ankle awhile, and you'll need help, whether from a nanny or domestic. I'm here, I'm strong, and I'm willing to work."

He slid his fingers to her ankle, probing muscles, palpating bones, drinking in the liquid velvet of her skin, the smooth warmth that beckoned a slower touch. She sucked in a violent breath.

"Hurt?" he asked.

"Of course it hurts," she snapped. "Anything hurts if you twist it hard enough."

"I didn't twist it, I touched it." He stared directly into her pain-filled eyes. "You've broken your ankle."

"No thanks to you."

"You're a little testy. Don't worry. We'll get you

fixed up in no time." Sliding one arm under her knees, the other behind her back, he lifted her against his chest.

"What are you doing?" Victoria stiffened, and winced.

"Taking you to a hospital." He walked toward the backyard, nestling her soft curves closer despite every notion that warned against it. "Your leg needs professional help."

"You need professional help. Get me an ice bag, and I'll be fine."

Gabe lowered her feet to the ground, allowing her to test her weight-bearing ability. She gasped, and her ankle wobbled. He anchored her to his side. *"Au contraire, mon frère,"* he quipped, his eyes twinkling with devilish delight. "I've seen plenty of broken bones." Hell, he'd given plenty of them. "And yours," he added, nodding at the swollen joint, "is definitely nasty. Any other questions?"

Victoria pressed her lips together. Gabe swung her back up in his arms. This time she looped a long, smooth arm around his neck. Her warm, moist breath wafted around his ear, sending an erotic shiver through him.

He clenched his teeth and fought back, even while admitting he liked it. Her round bottom rubbed his belly as he walked; she smelled clean, sunshine-fresh, and her ebony hair gleamed blue in the light. He'd wanted to get close, all right, but this was conducive to spontaneous combustion.

He carried her effortlessly, settling her into a comfortable position. "So," he pressed again. "Am I hired?"

She set her jaw and remained silent. Gabe ignored it and shouldered the backyard gate open. "Hey, guys," he called. Three sets of eyes trained on the woman in his arms.

They all spoke at once, and Gabe didn't know who said what when, but Victoria interpreted it all like a pro.

"I'm fine," she hastened to assure them. "At least I will be. Mr. Sanders has graciously—" Gabe heard her grind her teeth on the word "—consented to be our nanny, and his first job is taking me to the hospital."

Three sets of eyes zeroed in on him again, staring as if he'd arrived from another galaxy.

"I think your mom broke her ankle," he explained, shifting Victoria in his arms and fending off another shaft of heat. "Everybody slip on a T-shirt, and you can ride along."

"You're our nanny?" Anastasia asked. "For real?"

"Looks like it, short stuff," Gabe said, and hesitated, on unsure ground for once. He didn't want to use these kids.

Relishing the feel of Victoria filling his arms, Gabe knew he may be in over his head. He gazed down at Anastasia and regretted what was to come, but he'd do everything in his power to shield them as best he could. "Is that okay?"

Anastasia considered, glanced at her brother and sister, and bounced up and down. "Yippee!"

Jillian and Michael exchanged a high five, and Gabe realized the double-edged sword he sat on. "Come on," he ordered. "Let's move it. My car in five minutes. Mike, Jill, lock all the doors before you come out. You'll owe me a quarter for any one unlocked when we get back."

"I see command comes easily to you, Mr. Sanders," Victoria commented coolly.

Her sweet, low voice seduced his senses, and he

discovered he liked the sound of his name on her lips. "So?"

So Victoria knew she had no choice. Waves of throbbing pain nauseated her. He was probably right about the ankle being broken. Even if it wasn't, she'd need help. What a time for her options to run out.

"Very well." If she had to hire him, it would be on her terms. "My children are particularly vulnerable to you right now. You're the first man to live with them since their father died." She pinned him with intense maternal scrutiny. "Hurt them, and I'll never forgive you."

THREE

What little good humor Victoria had left was poked, prodded, and X-rayed out of her at the hospital. Her ankle wasn't broken, only badly sprained. She was systematically "braced and Aced" and wheeled down to the waiting room.

Her new nanny leaned a broad shoulder against the wall, a public telephone against his ear. "Yeah, well, don't call me at all. Not unless it's a damned emergency like life, death, or money."

An odd conversation for a nanny, she thought, but the hypo of Demerol she'd been given earlier left her groggy and confused. Perhaps she'd misheard.

Gabriel snatched a list of final instructions from the orderly wheeling her chair. "No driving, no walking, no crutches for the next ten days," he gloated. "Guess I'm not only the nanny, but the chauffeur, litter bearer, chief cook, and bottle washer. Okay, troops, let's book it."

Victoria tried to muster a glare, but fell short. Her children's confused gazes flew to Gabriel's.

39

"That means we're out of here, guys," he told them, and they all raced to the car.

He was gleeful, gloating, happy as any man who'd gotten his way. From the way he'd handled things so far, it looked as if he was excellent with children. But then, she thought with a smirk, he hadn't locked horns with any of them yet. Wait until he tasted a go-around with Jillian. Victoria had lost, and he'd won. But what was the prize?

Be careful what you wish for, Gabe's grandmother had always warned, *you just might get it*. And, boy, he had it!

He glanced around, assessing the large bedroom Victoria had assigned him. Ruffled pillow shams and bed flounces bore a muted but distinctly feminine touch. An air of disquiet settled around him, and he glared at the room's warm, spicy tones, so at odds with the bland decor of his own house.

Wrenching the draped lace curtain aside, he glowered into the well-manicured backyard. Damn! Everything'd seemed so simple when he'd talked to Rick. Find the fugitive and nail him. Gabe had done it countless times in countless ways. This case shouldn't be any different.

But it was.

This fugitive had an innocent family, children Gabe hated to involve. They didn't deserve a taste of the seamier side of life, but there was nothing he could do to prevent it. Except stay on the far perimeter of their lives. Alone and uninvolved, his two personal ground rules.

Hell, what case had ever been screwier, or scarier? Gabe would've rather faced a firing squad than scan the worshipful gazes of the Devereaux kids again. But face them he would, every morning, every afternoon, until

Hunter arrived. And then? Gabe could only imagine the condemnation he'd see in their eyes when it ended. His chin fell to his chest, and he spat out a whispered curse.

The situation required a clearer head and a cooler heart than he'd ever needed. He was well suited for it. He had to live with the Devereauxs without getting personally involved.

After one last trip to his place in Council Bluffs for incidental items, he'd be firmly entrenched. With a family, he noted with a frown. Those dreams had been wrenched away years ago. Now he was neck-deep in home and hearth, and discovered the dream hadn't died, not really. In an empty corner of his sterile heart, a dormant, unvoiced hope still thrived.

His decision was for the best, Gabe told himself. He wouldn't fit in here, not with this family. He didn't have the emotional energy to give of himself. Now wasn't the time to get caught up in useless desires. The case was booby-trapped, and he wanted as few scars as possible when he left.

For everyone.

A nanny in name only, a bondsman/bounty hunter by trade; he made money off other people's problems. He wasn't a nice guy and had no desire to change. Once he nabbed Hunter, Gabe would leave—hell, the Devereauxs would kick his butt out—and his life would get back to normal.

Normal? He shot a cynical glare at the queen bed with its shiny brass headboard and footboard. Classic. Cozy. Comfortable. Victoria's style, not his. His life was anything but normal to begin with, but after this? His fists clenched. He couldn't, wouldn't, get involved—

A deep stage sigh came from behind. Gabe frowned over his shoulder. "Yeah?" he barked.

A hesitant silence passed, and he spun around.

Clipped impatience vaporized. Anastasia, bottom lip quivering, shoulders slumped in marked dejection, stood in the doorway. She raised a dewy, pathetic gaze to him and heaved another sigh—heavier and shuddering. Gabe's intentions dissipated like dew in the sun. His heart hadn't heard a word.

"Nobody don't want us no more," Anastasia said, as if she'd lost her best friend in the world. Molly skulked up behind her. Nose pointed at the carpet, tail tucked between her legs, she mirrored her miniature mistress.

Something deep inside Gabe twisted with unnegotiable insistence. It would take a stronger man than he to resist Anastasia Devereaux.

Broadsided, caught unawares, all he could do at this point was surrender gracefully. Biting the inside of his cheek to keep a fond smile at bay, he crossed the room and knelt before the duo of doom. "You've got to be kidding," he said softly. "Who wouldn't want a cutie like you?"

" 'N Molly, too."

"Two cuties," Gabe corrected, and smoothed a silken lock of baby-fine hair out of her eyes.

"Mama's doing dumb old bookwork. Jill's talkin' on the phone to some dumb old boy from church," she recited, "and Michael and his friend don't want us around 'cuz we're dumb old girls."

Gabe's brows lifted in feigned surprise. "What a couple of chauvinists," he scoffed.

"Yeah," Anastasia heartily jeered. "What a bunch'a show-show-nests!" She glanced up at Gabe. "Do you want us?"

Gabe rested an elbow on one knee, and met his fate and the truth head on. He was a goner. "I think I'll always want you, short stuff," he whispered, and held out his arms.

Anastasia hurtled against his chest, wrapped her arms around his neck, and hugged him tight. "Forever and forever?"

God, was he out of his ever-lovin' mind? This was the high road to heartache, and here he was embracing it at full speed. But what else could he do?

He hugged her back. "Forever and forever," he whispered, and kissed the baby-soft skin behind her ear.

Okay, so he was dying here—but it was only with Anastasia. Nobody could resist such a wide-eyed, openly affectionate munchkin. She was young. Her wounds would have a better chance to heal with no scars, but that was it. No one else. No more ties. No more involvement.

Molly slinked up and nudged her cold, wet nose under his arm. Gabe tightened his hold on Anastasia and ignored Molly. The dog burrowed more insistently. Resigned to the inevitable, Gabe disengaged his arm and wrapped it around the animal's neck, pulling her into the embrace with a grudging groan. "All right," he groused. "But this is it, and that's final."

"This is what?" Anastasia asked.

"Uh, time to get moving. I've got to make one more trip to my house, and then I'll be back to stay."

"Forever and forever?"

Pain knifed through Gabe; he hadn't meant it to come out that way. "For as long as I can," he said in a husky voice, and ruffled her bangs. "Okay?"

She scrunched up her nose and grimaced. "Ah, phooey."

"I'll be back before you know it." He chucked her under the chin and stood up.

"Can we come, too?" Anastasia turned an Oscar-winning poor-little-me face to him.

He tunneled his fingers through his hair to knead the back of his neck. "I don't—"

"Don't you want us no more?" Her plaintive notes strummed his rusty heartstrings.

Her face fell a disheartened notch, and a resigned sigh filtered through his lips. "All right. Go ask your mom."

Immediately recovering herself, Anastasia clapped a hand over her mouth and giggled. "Yippee!" she cried, and raced down the hall, Molly loping close behind.

Gabe ambled along, bringing up the rear, trying to erase the sappy smile he knew wreathed his face.

What an idiot he was! Anastasia Devereaux didn't have a despondent bone in her gleeful little body. Hell, for all he knew, the dog was in on it, too.

Gabe had been royally had. And dammit, he couldn't remember enjoying anything more.

It was happening already, Victoria realized. As her worst fear unfolded before her eyes, she was helpless to stop it. With her foot propped up on a chair and a mountain of paperwork piled on her desk, she was totally powerless. Gabriel Sanders had landed in their lives like a summer tornado: fast and full of nonstop energy.

He'd insinuated himself into their lives as if it were the most natural thing in the world. He took to Anastasia's tea parties with an unnerving naturalness. Jillian hung on his every word like a novice with a guru. Michael glowed under each slight but encouraging nod of approval. Even Molly, that bastion of undying loyalty, had been won over with a rawhide bone and a scratch behind the ears.

He was wonderful to her, too, although Victoria hated to admit it. He insisted on carrying her wherever he thought she needed to be. She hated the helplessness her injury brought her almost as much as she hated her dependence on Gabriel.

If honesty was the best policy, she'd also have to admit he was a multitalented character. He commandeered her children with quasi-military expertise. He could be impervious, imperial, and unmoving, but he could also be warm, witty, and wonderful.

Victoria saw the writing on the proverbial wall. She was a big girl and had learned her lessons well. He wouldn't mean to hurt anyone, but it was inevitable. Living together brought companionship and closeness. Elements that produced happiness created profound pain, as well she knew.

Victoria worried most about Anastasia. She hadn't experienced the heartbreak of losing a loved one. She didn't remember her father's death; she'd been born two months later.

Now her daughter was attaching herself to Gabriel without any encouragement on his part, allowing Victoria a glimpse of the past and the future. Nannies were a lot like the men in her life. They'd leave her, just when she needed them most.

Voices drifted through the hall. Anastasia followed Gabriel into the house, regaling him with "kid humor," silly jokes with punch lines only her dog understood and only her mother laughed at.

"Knock, knock," Anastasia sang out.

Gabriel reached up and gently rapped his knuckles against the top of her head. "Knock, knock back to you," he said with a wide grin. "Enough's enough!"

"Ah, phooey," Anastasia replied. "What'cha wanna do, Gabe?"

Victoria held her breath, listening until their voices faded out of range. In their wake, a tomblike silence hung in her office. She had her hands full being two parents to three children. There was never enough of her to go around. Now Gabriel was in their lives, and the future had never looked so confused. All she wanted was to look after her mother and give her children a stable environment. Was that asking Providence for too much?

Victoria covered her face with her hands. Anastasia had bonded with Gabriel. It was only a matter of time before all three saw him as a major role model. Victoria had no idea how to stop it, even if she could.

"Mama?" a petite voice intruded.

Victoria dropped her hands to the desk and smiled into her youngest child's uncharacteristically somber eyes. "What is it, sweetheart?"

"Well . . ." Anastasia dropped her gaze to the floor. "Uh . . . me 'n Molly wondered if . . . if we could be Gabe's."

"Gabe's what, dear?"

"You know . . . Gabe's family."

A cold pang of hurt, followed closely by jealousy, pierced her heart. *No, you most certainly may not!* almost escaped Victoria's lips, but something in her daughter's downcast manner stayed her tongue.

This child was laughter and love, always upbeat and a joy to be around. What happened to so upset Anastasia's usual easygoing manner?

Victoria cleared her throat, leaned back in her chair, and held out her arms. Anastasia lunged onto her mother's lap, and Victoria nestled her close, wondering how best to approach the sticky subject with the least damage. "I love you, sweetheart. You know that, don't you?"

Anastasia nodded. "But nobody loves Gabe, Mama. He don't have nobody."

"Doesn't have anybody, dear," Victoria corrected.

"Yeah," Anastasia affirmed, and sat up to face her mother. "He lives all alone in a big, dark house. He don't have kids, or a mom, or a dad. There's nobody there to take care of him."

"Doesn't have," Victoria murmured absently. She'd known of his solitary existence from his resumé, but Anastasia painted a bleak picture. It shouldn't concern either of them how he lived his life. "He doesn't need anyone to take care of him. That's why I hired *him*, to take care of *you*."

Anastasia scanned her mother's office and pointed at various pictures. "He doesn't have none of those, an' his house is h-u-u-ge." She gestured with open arms outstretched. "It's real dark, too. Do you think he's scared to live there all by hisself?"

A memory stirred, then rattled. A recollection of their first meeting, his incredible hazel eyes and the pain she thought she'd imagined. Had Gabriel hurdled some emotional abyss? "I doubt anything scares Mr. Sanders, dear."

"But, Mama," Anastasia said more forcefully, as though her mother were missing the major point of the universe. "He's all alone, and we've got three kids. If he had me 'n Molly, he'd have two an' you'd still have two left over."

Victoria blinked a sudden moisture out of her eyes. Pride in Anastasia's compassion warmed her soul, but the request could never be. "Anastasia," she began, "I could never give you up."

"But, Mama, he's alone. Don't you feel sad for him?" her daughter pleaded. "If you let us be his, we'd come and see you, I promise."

Victoria choked a laugh through the thick lump in her throat. It was all so easy in a child's mind, black and white with no room for the murky gray that muddled an adult's.

Two notions settled on Victoria at once. First, Anastasia's mind was made up, and once that happened, there was no swaying her from the predetermined course. Two, it was already too late to protect her baby. All Victoria could do was stand aside, help pick up the pieces when it was over, and back out now as best she could. But not without giving it one more shot.

"Darling," she began. "Sometimes children get confused about a man they like very much, and they think he's their daddy. When he goes away, the children are very, very sad, and they hurt a lot in here." Victoria pressed her hand to her chest. "I'd feel bad if you hurt like that."

"Mama . . ." Anastasia sighed and lifted her shoulders in obvious exasperation with thickheaded adults. She drew her face nose to nose with her mother's. "He's *not* a daddy," she said slowly. "He's Gabe, and he needs us."

It was Victoria's turn to sigh. "Okay, I'll tell you what," she said. "You and Molly can be his special somebodies as long as he stays here, but that's all."

Anastasia opened her mouth as if to argue the point. Her gaze flew to the open door. Victoria's followed. Lounging lazily against the oak frame, Gabriel crossed his arms over his wide chest and cocked his head in a sparse but arrogant salutation. Such cheekiness only came with the Y chromosome, Victoria decided with a touch of asperity.

Anastasia shimmied off her mother's lap, planting a moist kiss on Victoria's cheek as she left. "Gabe,

Gabe," she cried, bounding across the room. "Guess what? Mama says we can be your somebodies."

Not we, Victoria wanted to correct, *you*.

Anastasia jumped up and down, clapping her small hands together. Long, dark pigtails brushed her nose, accompanying her enthusiastic "Isn't that great?"

The ghost of a smile tickled Gabe's mouth, and he gave the exuberant strands a playful tug. "Sure is, short stuff."

"Oh boy! Let's have a tea party."

"Anastasia, I need to speak with Mr. Sanders." Victoria wondered why the words tripped out in a breathless rush. He was her employee. A few moments alone should be nothing out of the ordinary, but with Gabriel, the air crackled and sparked as if she were skating on high-voltage wires.

"Ah, phooey," came her daughter's disheartened reply.

"I'll be out as soon as I'm done." Gabe cupped Anastasia's head in his large palm. "Okay?"

"Okay. See you later, alligator," she said and scampered off, her faithful pet loping at her heels.

"After while, crocodile," he said with a grin, and caught Victoria's raised brows. "She picked it up from the radio," he explained with a shrug.

Victoria's expression, wistful and slightly amused, told him nothing. "Have a seat, Mr. Sanders."

"Call me Gabe," he returned with a half grin.

She ignored it. "I want to go over my schedule for running the house. My boss has agreed I can do paperwork at home for now."

Gabe focused on Victoria's businesslike approach. Everything was well documented on an ice white sheet of paper, typed by a crisp black carbon ribbon. In complete opposition, her clothes—casual cutoffs and faded turquoise tank top—looked soft, touchable, and lived-in. Hot pink nail polish adorned ten bare toes. Gabe steeled himself against the immediate image of tonguing each one.

"Are you getting all this, Mr. Sanders?"

"Laundry on Monday," he recited, pushing other errant thoughts aside. "A bit old-fashioned, I think, but livable; housecleaning on Wednesdays and Fridays, and I believe you were talking about the lawn and yard work?"

Her disgruntled expression almost made him laugh. Her lips, just this side of petulant, rattled his cage but good. A man would climb to heaven for a taste of them, he thought. Or maybe find it there.

"As I was saying . . ." Aggravation threaded her voice.

An unusual twist of panic snaked through Gabe. Good Lord, he hadn't made it through a week without fantasizing about her!

He needed to scuttle the erratic—not to mention erotic—thoughts. He needed a cold shower, several maybe. He needed a frontal lobotomy! Whoa. Slow down. Think cool and calm.

Think of her in a completely different light! Think of her as a mother, a sister, an employer. Just don't think of her as a woman. Not a bright, intelligent woman, not a warm, sensuous woman. Never mind she was both.

Biting back a groan, he shoved his hand into his tight jeans pocket. Agitated fingers rummaged for his battered pack of smokes. With an inner sigh of relief—or rescue?—he withdrew a crumpled, but serviceable, cigarette.

Before he could locate a match, his fingers were suddenly, startlingly, empty. Victoria held his cigarette at arm's length, dangling it between thumb and forefinger like an offensive piece of garbage.

"You can't smoke," she said with a delicate wrinkle of her perfect nose.

That was it! Time to let the lady know how far the man could be pushed. "The hell I can't," he grated through clenched teeth. "I've done it for twenty years."

She settled herself in her chair. "You can't smoke in this house or around my children. Not only is it a filthy, unhealthy habit—"

Clenching his jaw, Gabe cursed his miserable misfortune for drawing this case, for knowing Rick and for owing the favor. "Why, you sanctimonious—"

Victoria gripped the edge of her desk with white knuckles. Her glare forestalled the rest of his sentence. "No, you listen to me. You backed me off the porch, gave me this sprained ankle, and insisted I hire you. You'll follow my rules in my house. Besides—" she flopped against the back of her chair like a balloon that'd lost its air "—Anastasia is allergic to smoke. It triggers asthma attacks. I almost lost her once." Victoria trailed off until she was murmuring to no one in particular. "So little . . . eighteen months. So soon after my husband's death."

She drew a shaky breath. "I can't risk it again." Her liquid gray eyes implored his understanding and tempered his annoyance. "I won't let you risk it, either."

He stared back, his addictive habit wrestling with his rusty conscience. The thought of Anastasia struggling for breath brought to mind another struggle for life, another tiny body laced with tubes and beepers, lying in a hospital bed. He knew what Victoria didn't. He knew the unfathomable heartache of losing a child. He'd never endanger Anastasia.

She'd wriggled through a tiny crack in his well-placed armor. It was fitting, somehow, that the smallest of the family had found her way in, like a tiny grain of sand in a tight, begrudging oyster.

Gabe glared at the floor. Okay, so the kid's health demanded he stop smoking. No problem. Hunter should arrive within the week. Gabe could last seven days without a cigarette. He leveled a look at Victoria that had backed down convicted felons.

She didn't flinch a muscle or an eyelash. Instead, she reclined in her butter-soft leather chair with a serene expression that turned his insides to mush.

"Okay then," he finally growled. Gabe cursed the stars that had crossed his life with Bruce Hunter's again. He'd take a pound of Hunter's flesh for each hour minus cigarettes.

"Feel free to smoke outside." Her full, pink lips tilted upward. "We don't want you passing out from withdrawal."

She was teasing him! Gabe found it subtly sexy. The twinkle in the depths of her gray eyes, the gentle lift of her lips, packed the punch of rocket fuel. If he spent much time around her, he'd turn into a blithering idiot.

Why'd she have to be so nice? He could deal with tough guys, the scum of the earth, or Victoria when she was stiff and formal. But when she turned warm and plain old nice, he faltered, then lost it completely.

Faint smudges rimmed her gray eyes, the only remnants of an obviously fitful night, pain pills or no. A deep pang of unwanted guilt rushed through him, reminding him how hard he'd pushed her. He wrestled against the unfamiliar emotion, put up a valiant struggle, and in the end, accomplished the unthinkable. An apology. "Look, about the past few days . . ."

"What about them?"

"I'm . . ." He grappled with the words. "I'm usually not so pushy," he lied, and for the first time in years, wished he weren't. Pushy or lying.

"And I'm usually not so stubborn."

He doubted it. When it came to her children, or those she loved, Gabe figured she'd be harder than steel.

"Can we hammer this out? A working relationship, Mr. Sanders? For the good of my children?"

Ebony hair fell around her shoulders and framed her face in soft curls. Sitting there, waiting for his answer, she looked so approachable, so touchable, and dammit all, so kissable! She reminded him of what he didn't want, what he couldn't have, what he'd lost.

"There's only one way to get along with me, Mrs. Devereaux," he said in an odd, throaty voice. His gaze melded with hers a long, knowing moment. Tension shimmered and arced between them. "Call me Gabe."

Victoria visibly relaxed and smiled. It slammed through him like bottled electricity. Thank God he wouldn't be here long. Anxious to put space between himself and Victoria, he pushed out of the chair.

"One other thing, Gabriel." Her soft, hesitant pronunciation of his name cut off further retreat.

"We're expecting my brother, Bruce, in the next two weeks. We don't know exactly when, but he's always hard to pin down. I hope it won't be an inconvenience."

Gabe's brows merged together. Two weeks with no cigarettes? Two weeks of cold turkey? Two weeks of living with Victoria?

"Bruce is wonderful. Outgoing, friendly, excellent with the children," she gushed. "They absolutely worship him."

Oh, great, fine and double dandy. Before busting Mr. Wonderful, he'd get to burrow into this family a little deeper, make his betrayal a little harder. His frown deepened.

"I think you'll like him," Victoria ventured.

Blast it! Damn Hunter and his lousy timing!

"Well, no matter," Victoria rushed on as he scowled in stony silence. "You can have those days off—"

"No!" Gabe shouted. Obviously startled by his sudden vehemence, Victoria snapped her head up. "I mean, no problem," he soothed. "In fact—" he bared his teeth in a wolfish smile "—I can't wait to meet him."

FOUR

Five days since she'd hired him, Victoria mused. Five whole days. Such a short time, yet a lifetime.

Comfortably situated in the shade of the table's giant umbrella, she succumbed to woolgathering. A pile of paperwork stared up at her, and she frowned at her inability to concentrate on figures and spreadsheets. Tapping her pen against her chin, she faced the thought dogging her.

In the past five days, Gabriel had managed to nudge his way into her home, her children's hearts, and her family's life with incredible ease.

Since her husband's death, Victoria had assumed innumerable burdens without realizing it. She hadn't known how heavy those responsibilities were until Gabriel barreled into her life. He lightened her load as though it were the most natural thing in the world. He saw, or sensed, what was needed, and accomplished it efficiently and succinctly.

While he was a welcome respite in dealing with her children, she also found him tolerable around the house.

55

He didn't grumble about never-ending dirty dishes, mountains of laundry, or the incessant role of judge and jury to three sparring siblings.

He'd shown intelligent adult conversation during the day, lighthearted teasing across the supper table, and companionable silence during the long evenings. His company was solid and reassuring. She was hardly capable of resisting him.

"Hey, Gabe!" Michael hollered from the pool's diving board. "Lookit this cannonball!" Cool water sprayed high as the boy's body battered the water. He surfaced seconds later, gasped, and hung on to the cement side. "How was that?"

Gabriel strode across the patio and stared down. With the soberness of an Olympic judge, he granted a slight nod of approval. "Super, kid. You're getting better."

Victoria's heart swelled, even as she bit her lip. Michael's eyes glowed with undeniable appreciation. Her son's reaction was always the same, radiating pleasure under Gabriel's constant and encouraging approval.

From the beginning, her children had seen an indefinable something in Gabriel. They'd adopted him on sight. But she sensed an aloofness, as though he wasn't an easy mixer. He wasn't quick to smile, either, but when he did, it softened the hard, chiseled planes of his face to almost handsome.

She doubted anyone would ever label him classically good-looking. His dark features were too intense, his tall, broad-shouldered build too overwhelming. But he was a man who drew the eye. Especially a woman's.

His damn-the-establishment hair beckoned a lingering touch. Although casual clothes hid his lean body, Victoria's memory contained every heart-stopping detail of what lay beneath today's red Mickey Mouse T-shirt and snug khaki shorts. She couldn't live with another human without meeting him in various stages of dress, and partial undress. He was as imposing physically as he was in personality.

Sensing a softer layer beneath the rock-hard exterior, her children weren't awed or put off by him in any way. A slight but perpetual frown, as if he constantly analyzed the world and found it lacking, didn't faze them.

Victoria discovered the same indefinable quality that drew her brood to Gabriel lured her, also. She even smiled at her children's enthusiastic narratives, hotly peppered with "Gabe says" and "Gabe thinks."

Gabriel, too, had a special glow around her kids. In his gruff, masculine way, he liked them, and anyone who liked her dog and kids had wonderful taste.

Still, she was torn between wanting a stable family life and wanting to shield them from possible hurt.

Don't borrow trouble.

His resumé showed a stable track record. Two years with each previous employer wasn't bad, and now he was near his Iowa home, which had been the reason for leaving his last employer. Maybe the Devereauxs would do better. If he grew to love the kids, he might stay longer.

Grow up, Victoria. When was love ever enough?

She castigated herself as an idiot and shoved her work into a briefcase. If Gabriel had her daydreaming about a nebulous future, she was going soft between the ears.

He ducked under the tilted umbrella and braced his long arms against the tabletop. "Lunch is ready."

Pulling her sunglasses down the bridge of her nose in a manner she hoped was condescending and would give her some breathing room, she eyed him speculatively. "I didn't hear the smoke alarm."

"Very funny, Mrs. Devereaux," he drawled in a serious tone, and sauntered closer. "Those who complain do dishes."

Pointing to the ankle he'd propped atop three pillows earlier, she shrugged. "Can't."

He sidled next to her, his hair-dusted thigh brushing against her knuckles. "Sure you could." His deep baritone growl vibrated through every nerve in her body. "I'll hold you up." He leaned back, obviously sizing her up. "About five foot ten to my six one?" he asked himself.

Victoria's cheeks flushed with heat. How many times and on how many women had he honed those evaluation skills to such precision? "Close."

Before she could draw her next breath, he ran a finger along the curve of her jaw in a quick, soft glide. "God, what a fit we'd be."

A chuckle rumbled out of him and curled her toes. The first semblance of a laugh she'd heard from him totally captivated her. No wonder her children followed him around like the Pied Piper of Ponca Hills.

Michael launched himself out of the pool, scattering crystal water droplets in his wake, and provided a much-needed reality check. Gabe jerked back and frowned.

What magic did this family weave? Every day brought more ties, invisible silken ropes binding him closer to each one. Victoria's munchkins refused to let him sit around uninvolved.

Only an ogre could ignore those cherubic faces. Far be it from Gabe to deny them. The trouble was, the more he gave, the more they drew him out. He wasn't their parent, a fact they could quickly make him forget.

Victoria was a helluva good mother, long on patience and nurturing, short on any faults he could see. He had to admit he was drawn to her. Circe couldn't have tempted Ulysses more than Victoria lured Gabe. An aura of alluring femininity coupled with her loving, nurturing side created more sizzle than a side of breakfast bacon.

Gabe was already hooked on the quiet evening hours when she read to Anastasia and Michael. Her voice drizzled around him like warm honey, and fond memories from his own childhood surrounded him.

In dealing with the I-know-everything-I'm-almost-a-teenager Jill, Victoria showed extraordinary patience. In Victoria, Gabe sensed a healing balm, and like a mongrel drawn to food, he eased down his guard and crept closer.

Which proved how dangerous she was. Not in a criminal way. God knew he'd tried to find a shred of evidence that implicated her in her brother's scheme, but came up empty-handed.

Victoria was no black widow. He almost wished she were. That territory, he knew too well. No, Victoria radiated softness and love. Her attraction came from the essence of what she was. Simply a woman.

Only there was nothing simple about Victoria, or the feelings she fostered in him.

Something cold and wet palmed his sun-heated thigh. Gabe spun around. "What the h—"

A moment's fear flashed through Anastasia's clear, gray eyes. Gabe cursed himself a daydreaming dolt and immediately softened, crouching beside her on bended knee. "Sorry, short stuff. You scared me."

Instantly forgiving, she hugged him. "Mama says you're not scared of nothin'," she reported loftily.

Gabe angled a glance at Victoria, unable to hold back a grin. "Does she, now?" he drawled. Funny your mama's the one thing that does scare me.

"I'm hungry," Anastasia announced. "Where's lunch?"

"Yeah," Michael chimed in. "I could eat a horse."

"I could eat a lion," Anastasia countered, her pert nose lifting two notches.

"Well, I could eat a hippopotamus," Michael called back.

"And I could eat an elephant," the youngest insisted.

"Oh yeah? I could eat your dumb ol' dog," her brother supplied with an evil grin. "Where is Molly?"

Anastasia shrieked. Victoria hid a smile behind her hand. Unruffled, Gabe shook his head. "Enough already."

"You wouldn't let him eat Molly, would you, Gabe?" Anastasia turned a worried gaze up to him.

He tugged affectionately on her dripping ponytail. "Never, ever. but he's getting an Alpoburger if he doesn't lay off." He swung her off her feet with a big tickle. She giggled; he grinned. "Lunch is served in the kitchen."

"Okay." She skipped across the flagstone and hopped through the door.

Gabe turned back to Victoria. She stared at him with a perplexed frown knitting her brows, and something else. Something that brought a shaft of warmth crashing through his belly, something that scared the hell out of him, something that pulled at him like the very devil. "The natives are restless," he said, not knowing what else to say.

"Downright ornery," she agreed.

"Michael's a good kid. Boys get pretty squirrelly around age eight."

"When do they grow out of it?" she asked softly, watching him in a way that twisted his stomach in a square knot.

"Somewhere around thirty-five," he quipped, hoping to lighten the conversation.

She laughed. Instead of cooling him, it heated him up. God, he'd kill to wrap himself up in those husky, throaty tones. They surrounded him, slid over his skin like warm sable. In a heartbeat, the air between them shimmered.

Could she feel it?

He didn't wait to find out. Move. Do something. Anything. Just don't lean down and taste those dusky, parted, waiting lips.

"Mother!"

Gabe jumped. Victoria lurched. Attention riveted on the open French doors, where Jill held out a cordless phone. "The nursing home,' she announced. "Something about Grandma."

Victoria stared at her mother's pale, drawn face. Congestive heart failure. Mini stroke. She'd learned more about medicine in the past months than she cared to know.

The doctor slung the stethoscope around his neck. "I wish the news was better, Mrs. Devereaux. Her heart wasn't strong to begin with. Now it's enlarged."

Victoria sighed and scrubbed her forehead.

"We're doing everything we can. She's responding to the medication, and should be back in the nursing home by week's end."

Victoria nodded and shouldered the invisible burden without comment. There was nothing to do but play out the hand Fate had dealt.

The doctor speared her with a cursory glance at her ankle. "You could use some looking after, too. Go home. She's going to be pretty sedated today, anyway."

Victoria nodded, and the physician swept out of the room. Clasping her mother's bony hand, she rubbed the thin, papery, skin, willing the situation to be different.

Why did life have to be so hard? Why did she have to be so useless to those she loved? "Bruce is coming, Mama," she told the older woman. "You know how he always cheers you up. He'll be here soon. We'll play cards . . . like we used to. . . . It'll be super. . . ."

A large, warm hand cupped her shoulder, communicating reassurance and strength. She smiled and placed her hand atop Gabe's. "Thank you for driving me."

He almost smiled. "You were hardly in any shape to do it. And the doctor's right."

"About what?"

"You need some looking after. I think you've taken care of everyone else for quite a while."

"Comes with the territory," she returned. "My husband died, my mother got sick, so I picked up and carried on."

"You've done a great job. I know a lot of people who would've folded under similar circumstances."

"Don't pin any medals on me yet."

"I'm not. You've borne the single-parent burden long enough. You can rest on your laurels as long as I'm around."

"How long will that be?"

"Nothing lasts forever. You know that." He glanced away and then back. "But I'm here now."

His statement struck her as odd, foreboding, but she couldn't figure out why. He was right. Nothing lasted forever. No one knew that better than she, and yet having him near during this latest crisis felt more than good, more than secure. It felt comfortable. For now it was enough. "Let's go home."

Home. Gabe lit a cigarette and sat under the huge sugar maple in Victoria's backyard. The kids were asleep, a soft, humid breeze sifted through his hair, and Victoria was in her bedroom reading. *Let's go home.*

He drew deeply off the cigarette and blew the smoke to the leaves. Molly strode up and sniffed at his hand in apparent disdain. "You're in the right household," Gabe muttered. Even his cigarettes didn't have the same zing as before. Before Victoria. Before this *home.*

He stubbed three quarters of the nicotine stick out and flicked it away. Molly edged closer, and Gabe scratched her behind the ears. "What the hell have I gotten myself into, girl?" His hand stilled as his mind raced. "And why can't I let it ride?"

The dog nudged his quiescent hand. "Yeah, yeah, Your Majesty. So how about a little input? What is it about those kids that I can't turn my back on?" Molly scooched closer, resting her head on his thigh. Gabe's hand slowed, smoothed along her short blond fur. "What is it about their mother? I don't want to leave her alone, but I can't really pursue her either. Can I? I mean, in all good conscience, I shouldn't."

Her words echoed in his head. *Home.*

That was the problem. He was starting to feel at home. Once he did, how would he leave it behind?

Victoria wasn't reading, she was worrying. She rubbed circles over her pounding temples. It was happening to her. Gabriel Sanders was slipping through her defenses, slowly but surely. She should know better.

But, oh! The comforting shoulder to lean on today had been heaven. He hadn't expected her to be strong, always on, ready to fight a battle. He'd taken care of her.

Empathy was the man's middle name. When he'd carried her into her mother's room and settled her in a standing position, he'd reached out and smoothed a lock of white hair off her mother's forehead. He possessed infinite gentleness and fought hard to cover a sensitive nature.

Gabriel Sanders. Enigma. Paradox. Old-fashioned male. He did what he wanted, when he wanted and how he wanted, but there was a heart of solid gold behind it.

The cool, crusty character, she could deal with. But with disarming unpredictability, Gabriel occasionally cracked a seam in his impenetrable shell and let a bit of humanity peek out.

The nanny she'd hired to care for her children answered needs of her own, cravings she almost forgot existed. Gabriel had definitely rattled her well-ordered existence.

A splash drew her to the bay window. He was out for a moonlight swim. She turned out her reading lamp and watched in covert silence, staring to her heart's content.

He was a magnificent specimen. The low-slung, high-cut scrap of spandex left no doubt that he was one well-put-together male. Not that she hadn't noticed from the moment she'd seen him, but live, up close, and, Dear Lord, bare-chested, he was something else altogether.

Masculine. Virile. *Sexy*.

Oh, yes, an inner voice whispered. *Definitely sexy*. To the max, as Jillian would say. His broad-shouldered presence could suck the air from her lungs, or shrink a room in no time flat. He launched himself out of the pool, water clinging to the dark thicket of chest hair that spread across his well-formed but not overly muscled pectorals. A narrow, silken strip of hair disappeared into the spandex. Her fingers itched to explore it. He sauntered toward his towel looped over the chaise, fascinating her with his long-legged, gait. A strange tickle formed beneath her rib cage.

"Hey, babe. What's up?" he called.

Victoria stopped breathing, moving, or thinking. Had he seen her playing junior voyeur? An immediate bark restarted her heart.

Gabriel planted his palms on his lean hips, dipping the swim trunks just below his tan line. "Well, come on," he told the dog with a hint of boyish petulance.

Molly jumped into the water, and Gabriel dove in after. Victoria couldn't keep a fond smile from her lips . . . or from her heart. A man with time for kids and dogs, and who wanted to take care of her. If that didn't take the proverbial cake.

She'd brought an efficient, competent, well-mannered—albeit a bit pushy—man into her home. One with the smile of a scamp, the voice of an angel, and a body to rival Tom Selleck.

He was hard to resist. If she blocked him out on one level, he sneaked in on another. He'd carried her wherever she needed, or didn't want, to go. In his arms, she was engulfed in solid comfort, enveloped in a companionable cocoon that made her want to curl up and stick around a long while. His palm seemed to scrape against her thighs in a sensuous rasp. Each time he picked her up, uncontrollable heat, accompanied by a sudden shiver, flashed up her spine and down her arms. She hoped he hadn't noticed.

An hour later, Gabe sought Victoria's window. The light was off. She must be asleep already. What a sight she'd make, Gabe thought. All that black hair spread out on a white pillow, her beautiful skin glowing with that natural luminescence a Hollywood actress would envy.

Her body was to die for. Long and slender in all the right places, rounded and soft in the best places. With a resigned sigh, Gabe finally acknowledged what he'd fought so hard against.

He was drowning in her.

The most he could hope for was that Hunter would kick his backside in gear and get there. The worst was if he fell for Victoria while living the lie. He didn't want that, didn't want to create an inch of pain for her.

The one thing he wanted—no, dammit, demanded—was a taste of the good life. More than that, he wanted to bathe in it, drown in it, drink it in, and soak it up. Most of all, he wanted to hoard every moment like a miser.

Everyone deserved a little warmth in their lives.

Even a predator like him.

Victoria squeezed emotions from him he thought he'd buried with his wife and daughter. Victoria offered solace, relief for his battered soul.

As surely as the tide sought the shore, Gabe longed to seek out Victoria. But for her sake and his sanity, he had to keep his distance.

He only hoped he was equal to the task.

FIVE

Secluded on the patio, Victoria closed her eyes and inhaled, filling her lungs with the sweet scent of rain-laden air. In her youth, her California cousins had laughed at the idea that anyone could "smell rain." And yet, she had, could, and did. It was indescribable. The fresh, clean fragrance of impending moisture filled the atmosphere. Dark thunderheads, so familiar during a Nebraska summer, slowly drew together on the far horizon. Soft, cool breezes caressed her face and threaded through her unbound hair.

If she hadn't been immobilized by her irksome ankle, she might've missed the twilight and the heady aroma of oncoming rain. As it was, Gabriel had insisted on putting the younger children to bed—after all, he'd added with a slow wink that sent her heart into a trip-hammer pace, he *was* the nanny. Jillian had comman-deered the telephone for who knew how long, leaving Victoria completely alone for the first time in . . . dear Lord, in years.

She sighed and stretched in the chaise lounge, drink-ing in the balmy weather and solitude of the evening.

"Mind if I smoke?"

The rich, full baritone snapped her into a sitting position. She stared into Gabriel's incredible hazel eyes. In return, his gaze roamed over her loose hair, her eyes, nose, and chin with unhurried ease. She fought the urge to fidget, focusing on his square jaw and wide cheekbones. The man was altogether too virile for his good, or her sanity.

One side of his mouth hiked up with mild amusement. "Well, do you?"

"Oh!" Snap out of it, Victoria. Gawking at the nanny, her employee, for heaven's sake, wasn't quite appropriate. Even if he was the sexiest specimen to come down the pike in ages, had the shoulders of an NFL linebacker, and possessed the smile of a Regency rake. "No," she said, hating the breathlessness of her voice. "Go right ahead."

He nodded, patted his shirt pocket, and fished out a package of filtered menthols. Victoria watched, mesmerized by his long fingers tapping the pack against his opposite palm, his teeth drawing out a lone cigarette. Good grief, he was only smoking a cigarette, not doing a striptease.

But he made the simplest task ooze with sensuality. Like fishing a match out of tight Levi's, cupping large hands to keep the breeze away, or inhaling until his chest strained against his green polo shirt.

A hypnotist couldn't have put her under a more potent spell. He drew on his cigarette again, and blew a smoke ring. Nothing had ever been sexier. The man was simply a wizard. With the house, the children, and unfortunately, with her.

"Looks like rain," he said, breaking the comfortable quiet.

"Smells like rain," she countered, testing him against her unimaginative cousins.

He laughed, a breathtaking smile stealing across his face. "I haven't heard that in years. Not since my mother."

Victoria relaxed and settled back again. "That's where I always heard it, too. My mother."

"I'm sorry," he said, and she understood what he meant: her mother's health problems. He hadn't mentioned it since leaving the hospital, but his solid hand on her shoulder then had communicated solace and compassion in a way mere words could not. And oh! but it felt good to share the burden—if only for a moment—with another human being.

Oblivious to her thoughts, he continued. "It's hell watching someone you love just fade away."

She drew a deep, bracing breath and marveled at his words. He sounded as if he'd been there. "Yes, it is. What about you? When did your mother die?"

He inhaled again, studied the cigarette in a detached, thoughtful manner, and exhaled on a deep sigh. "About ten years ago. Cerebral hemorrhage. Went just like that," he said with a snap of his fingers. "Never had a chance to save her. Never got the chance to say goodbye."

It was Victoria's turn to sigh. "There isn't an easy way to lose a loved one. Quickly or slowly. It's pure hell any way you cut it."

He smiled at her. Not a full-blown heart wrencher, but a soft, slight smile as though he'd discovered something warm and wonderful. "You're one helluva woman, Victoria."

She shifted, glancing away. "Why? Because I care about my mother and children? That comes with the territory of being a daughter and a mother. There's nothing heroic about that.''

"Maybe, maybe not. There's a lot of mothers and daughters out there that tear each other up physically and emotionally. They shred their families and screw up their children. Sometimes going on with your life, doing the best you can in a lousy situation, is heroic. Not everyone can.''

Victoria heard the pain, the longing. Somewhere along the line, Gabriel had tripped over a mountain of heartache. She wanted to reach out, hold him close, and tell him everything would be all right. She settled for "You're not so bad yourself, Mr. Sanders.''

His head snapped up, a teasing twinkle lighting his eyes. "I thought you'd never notice, Mrs. Devereaux.''

She shook her head and laughed. "You're doing very well with your smoking, too.''

"You mean my nonsmoking?''

She chuckled her agreement. "A rose by any other name,'' she quipped. "I haven't noticed you snapping at the kids or me, or any of the nasty things people say happens when you go cold turkey. Truly, you've been—''

"A paragon of virtue?'' he asked, and waggled his brows.

"Not quite. You're far too pushy to be a paragon, but I like what I've seen so far. You have a softness around my children that I didn't expect when I interviewed you.''

"Good thing for me you're no sexist.''

"Good thing for me you're so tenacious,'' she countered.

"Yeah,'' he said quietly. "Real good. For us both.''

Before she could dwell on his cryptic comment, a fat,

cold drop of rain splotched on her nose. She reached to wipe it off when two more hit the back of her hand.

"Here comes the deluge." Gabriel bent to scoop her into his arms and cradle her against his warm, solid chest.

He'd carried her wherever she'd needed to go for the past ten days, and yet the solace she'd discovered in his embrace caught her by surprise each time he touched her. She stared at the open vee of his shirt; the springy curls teased her with what lay beneath the fabric. Lord, but he'd tempt a statue!

Tomorrow she'd be able to walk again. He'd still have chauffeur duty due to her restricted driving, but no more "litter bearing," as he'd nicknamed the sidelight.

A pity, she thought, and looped both arms around his neck. She'd gotten used to this, to him, to the wonderful sensation of his strength and presence. She'd miss him, and the comfort of the only person who'd wormed his way close to her in a very long time.

Carrying her into the house, Gabe didn't want to put her down. Or let her go. Every night had been the same. Tonight was no different. His arms tightened, but he forced the tension from his limbs.

Involvement, no matter how delightful or attractive the lady, wasn't part of the game plan. He'd repeated the litany throughout long days and longer nights.

Once into the shelter of the house, Gabe slowed his steps. Victoria settled back into the hollow of his damp shoulder.

Funny how she seemed to be made to fit right there. Although he'd joked and teased her about it, carrying Victoria was the best part of the job.

They'd been forcibly acquainted in a short period of time, but Gabe liked what he'd found in her. Physically she was a lightweight, but what little weight there was settled in all the right places. Nice, tightly rounded fanny. Skin smooth as Chinese silk. Every time he lifted her, he caught a scent that was half perfume, half Victoria, and all woman.

He didn't want to put her down now. He never did.

What he wanted was to carry her to his room and see if she tasted as good as she looked. If she was cool as a cucumber beneath the outward exterior, or if it was a facade covering the slumbering, sizzling sensuality he surmised was the real Victoria Devereaux.

Under different circumstances, he would. But not now. Not with this case. Not with this woman. She didn't know his rules of noninvolvement and emotional distance. She'd expect love and commitment, as well she should.

Not for the first time, Gabe wished those qualities were his to give. They weren't. Hadn't been for longer than he cared to remember.

He turned and headed up the stairs, carrying her like a precious commodity. Without a word, he deposited her on the end of her four-poster bed and headed toward the master bath.

"Um . . . you don't need to do that tonight," she called out.

He cocked a knee and planted his hands on his hips. "Why not? I've done this every night. This is ten in a row. Why's it different?"

"Oh . . ." She stared at the bedspread, smoothing it under her long, slim fingers. "No reason. I thought we could skip it. I mean, I'm getting my walking papers tomorrow."

Incredulous recognition of the reason for her hesitation dawned, and he stopped and turned back to her. "You're embarrassed? After all this time?"

She frowned at him. "Of course not."

His wide knowing grin said otherwise. "Wanna try it without the swimsuit tonight?"

Her brows climbed, an endearing flush staining her cheeks. She tossed a tasteful pillow sham at him. "Oh, for heaven's sake, go run the water!"

He laughed and flourished a bow. "Your wish is your lowly litter bearer's command."

Pouring a long dose of hellishly sexy-smelling oil into the steaming water of the hot tub, Gabe gritted his teeth. The scent evoked images of cool sheets and hot desire. "You're a crazy dude," he muttered. "One hundred percent looney-tuned."

Clenching his jaw against a rush of potent lust, he cursed himself again. He should be putting more distance between them, not drooling over her bath.

But he couldn't pry himself away from the images his imagination conjured. The sighs, splashes, and delicate scents were enough to make him run out into the chilly storm for a dose of cold reality.

This was a dream, nothing more. An erotic, sensual dream centering around the woman who waited at the end of her bed. He left her in the steamy bathroom, and practically bolted from the room.

He closed the door and leaned his head against it, listening to the rustle of clothes moving and dropping. She made his palms sweat.

Every night he'd deposited her on the vanity stool, leaving her to her own devices. Every night he'd spent a long, hard half hour waiting, listening, absorbing the sensual feast. Every night he had to endure retrieving her clean, damp body, knowing she didn't have much on under that robe.

It was a test of the outer fringes of his endurance and patience, and he wouldn't have denied himself a moment. If nothing else, he knew Victoria wasn't exactly immune to him.

Her satiny dressing gown caressed her breasts, the indentation of her waist, and the bell of her hips like an ardent lover. No way could she fool him.

One glance from him, no matter how brief or cursory, knotted her nipples and sent a shudder through her. It was all he could do to leave her alone to dress.

"Gabriel?" she called. "Are you there?"

"Yeah." His voice was thick and husky. "I'm here."

"I'd like to get into the Jacuzzi sometime this century. Are you ready?"

Oh, yeah, he conceded with a roll of his eyes. He was more than ready.

Gabe paced and waited. Waited and paced, and not with good humor. Unrelenting desire had a way of affecting him that way. He stared around the room, his gaze focusing on the chest of drawers. He ran his hand along the oak surface he'd polished two days ago. Opening the top right-hand drawer, he whistled long and low. Not that he hadn't known what he'd find. Doing a woman's laundry, a guy got to know her literally inside out.

This morning he'd almost lost his mind and his voice. Folding and sorting Victoria's underwear was a hellish ordeal in self-control. Now that he'd reverently laid those scraps and strings of lace-trimmed satin and silk into her cedar-scented drawers, he'd die to see them on her in person.

He fingered a lacy thigh-high silk stocking; a sigh slid through his lips. God, he'd bet she was a knockout in this stuff. His finger skimmed over a pale pink garter belt, shiny tap pants, and something that looked like an old-fashioned merry widow.

In black, of course. Others were red, hot pink, and virginal white. It was enough to raise his blood pressure and a whole lot more. Her unmentionables were the stuff long, hot summer dreams were made of.

Damn! If her brother didn't get there soon, Gabe'd lose every living marble he had left.

"Gabriel?"

His hand pulled back as if he'd been caught in a clandestine activity. He glared at the bathroom door. What sweet hell he'd put himself in. He was in too far to willingly back out, and yet didn't dare go forward. "Be right there," he called back.

Bumping the drawer shut with his hip, Gabe readjusted the fly of his straining Levi's. "Give me a minute."

Within moments, he had her out of the tub and bundled in a royal blue towel that covered her from nose to toes. He held her in the cocoon until she wriggled her mouth free. "Are you trying to smother me?"

"Sorry," he said, and swung her into his arms again. The short distance from the bath to her bed was mere feet, but it loomed in front of Gabe like the Grand Canyon.

Victoria wiggled in his arms, her fanny burrowing against his palm. "Have you lost your mind?" she asked.

Hell, yes. Why else would he torture himself? "Sorry again," he said, and plopped her on the bed.

Inky hair hung around her face. "You look like a drowned rat," he said.

"Thanks so much," she returned. "Get me my comb, and I'll remedy the situation immediately."

Gabe grabbed the wide-toothed comb from her bureau. Not stopping to evaluate his next action, he perched behind her and drew it from crown to ends.

Working the comb through the strands, he memorized the contour of her head, the slant of her nape, the curve of her ear.

Over and over, he slid the comb through her hair. Over and over, she sighed with a purr.

Gabe caught her shoulders, wanted to pull her into his arms, but instead placed her away from him. "I'd better go."

Her gaze tangled with his, and Gabe held his breath at what he saw. Gratitude, pure and simple, and a warmth that knew no bounds. It was both exciting and frightening as hell.

"It's been a long time since anyone's done that for me," she said simply. "It was wonderful. Thank you."

It had been his pleasure. She owed him no thanks. "Good night, Victoria."

Her smile was bittersweet, like the longing that welled up in Gabe. "Yes, good night."

Hesitating only a moment, Gabe could no more have stopped his next action than he could've flown off the statehouse. His lips touched her forehead, damp from the bath. He kissed the tip of her nose, waiting for her withdrawal.

None came.

He lowered his head, his lips brushing hers. Her breath caught, and she leaned closer to kiss him back with such incredible sweetness, it wrenched Gabe's heart.

Cupping her head in his palm, he strummed his thumb along her cheek. She turned in to it like a stray kitten. "Ah, Victoria," he whispered. "You turn me inside out."

Surprise lit her eyes. "I do?"

"Yeah," he chuckled, and planted a kiss on the top of her wet hair. "You sure do." Reaching across the bed, he snared the satin chemise she wore at night and tossed it in her lap. "Sweet dreams, sugar."

Gabe stalked out and closed the door, leaving the room, the woman, and his sanity behind.

Victoria's gaze followed him. She touched her fingers to her lips, still warm from his. She hadn't wanted him in her home, but he'd barged in anyway. So much had happened in such a short time, she didn't know what to think anymore. He turned her life upside down, inside out, and hung it out to dry.

She was tired of fighting herself on the subject of Gabriel Sanders. Totally exhausted, as a matter of fact.

Which would explain why she'd allowed his kiss.

Oh, right. In your dreams.

Exactly where she'd relive the magic of his touch, his lips, his kiss. In her dreams.

Lightning flashed in silver circuits across the black sky. A noisy storm and a nanny who could comb her hair out or kiss her with an exquisite gentleness that strummed her heart wouldn't allow her much sleep.

Dropping the towel, Victoria slipped out of the wet suit, into the multiprint chemise, and climbed under the sheet. It was going to be an extremely long night.

Someone was in his room.

Gabe's eyes popped open, scanning through the darkness as best he could. His right hand inched across the sheet and under the adjacent pillow. His weapon wasn't there!

Something cold and wet touched his bare shoulder, and he shot straight up, the sheet pooling around his waist. His hand snaked out and captured a small body, pulling it close.

"G-Gabe!" The whisper came through chattering teeth.

"Anastasia?" He flicked on the bedside lamp and squinted at her. "You're soaked—"

"C-come on," she said with a shudder that quaked through her body. Grabbing his hand, she tugged but didn't budge him. "H-hurry. Molly needs us."

"Hold on, short stuff." He lifted her up and wrapped her in the bedspread, chafing her arms and back with the dry material. "What's going on?"

"M-Molly's doghouse. The roof b-blew off an' sh-she was c-crying. She's hurt, 'n bleeding blood all over."

Gabe swung his legs over the side and grabbed his jeans. Good thing he'd had the foresight to sleep in his underwear since moving in. Nothing worse than nosy little females or compromising positions. He'd determined from the start not to be caught by the first, or in the second.

He shoved his legs into the denim, dispensing with the snaps. Lifting the cocooned Anastasia in one arm, he strode down the hall, stopping in Victoria's room.

Shouldering the door open without knocking, he deposited Anastasia beside her mother and tucked her close.

"What is it?" Instantly awake, Victoria flicked on her light.

His tucking motions on Anastasia stilled. It was all he could do to keep his mouth from dropping open in awed worship. If Gabe had thought Victoria irresistible earlier, he hadn't seen anything yet. Now, with a slumberous haze over her eyes, her white shoulders gleaming like marble cream in the soft light, she was simply mesmerizing.

Her gaze shifted from Gabe to Anastasia and back again. "What's going on?" she asked with a worried frown.

First things first, he admonished himself. First, take

care of the problem. Second, take care of your libido. "The doghouse. Anastasia thinks Molly may be hurt."

"Not maybe, Gabe," Anastasia pronounced as though adults were the densest creatures on the planet. "She's *bleeding* an' crying. *Please,*" she urged. "We've gotta help her."

"I'll check it out." He stood and locked his hands on his hips. "Stay here. *You*—" he pointed to Anastasia—"stay warm, and *you*—" he pointed to Victoria "—stay put."

Outside, wind-driven rain pelted the house with a stinging force. Gabe grabbed a windbreaker from the back room and turned on the floodlights. In the illumination he noted the roof had indeed blown off the doghouse and now lay upside down in a nail-wielding heap.

A long cry followed by a solitary "woof" came from a far corner of the pen. Molly was backed up against the fence, buffeted by the onslaught of the storm. Blood oozed down her forehead, cheek, and muzzle. Her large white teeth were bared in a snarl of confusion, and her hackles stood on end.

In the shadows, Gabe couldn't tell what was blood and what was rain, but he knew she was injured badly. It didn't look good.

Spotting him, the animal lifted forlorn amber eyes like a penitent to a savior, and another pocket in Gabe's heart filled to overflowing. This family wouldn't let up until they had him hook, line, and sinker. And he kept right on tugging at the bait. Oh, what the hell. What was another nibble? "All right, mutt. Let's go."

He hefted the dog's weight into his arms, moving slow and easy, and headed toward the house. Molly lay still and docile, her trust and love apparent in her manner. "Don't get too used to this," Gabe groused.

As if in answer, Molly laid her chin in the crook of his arm.

"Good," Gabe said, and squinted against the water streaming down his face. "As long as we've got it straight."

Inside the house, lights blazed. Anastasia zipped from window to window, peering out into the storm. Gabe spotted her as he stepped through the French doors. She sprang toward him, grabbing him around the knees. "How is she?"

Molly tried a pathetic wag of her tail. Gabe managed a sympathetic smile at the dog and the child. "I thought I told you to stay put and stay warm."

Anastasia shifted from foot to foot. "Mama said if I changed clothes, I could wait for you."

"Yes" came Victoria's voice from the kitchen. "I did."

His gaze shifted from mother to daughter, evaluating them both and liking what he saw way too much. "Neither one of you follows directions worth diddly-squat," he said with a scowl.

Victoria hobbled a few steps behind. "Must be her mother's daughter."

"Yeah, well, as long as you both understand who's boss."

Anastasia and her mother exchanged a conspiratorial wink and a smug smile. "Oh," Victoria said, "believe me. We do."

Spotting the other two kids on the steps, Gabe turned his attention to the injured dog. "Mike," he called. "Get me two old bath towels on the double."

"Jill, get an old blanket. Molly's starting to shake, and I don't want her going into shock."

Moments later, Gabe's pristine kitchen floor sported splotches of blood, water, and mud. The dog's shaking had quieted, but her injuries needed professional care. "Lucky the cuts weren't another eighth of an inch higher, or she'd have put out an eye."

Victoria shuddered and sank into a chair. Gabriel had everything well in hand. His large fingers, liberally peppered with dark hair, rubbed comfort and kindness into Molly's bedraggled fur. Although his exterior was gruff, brusque at times, the man had an inordinate capacity for love, for tenderness, for consideration.

"I'll take her to the emergency animal clinic," Gabe told her. "She needs those cuts cleaned."

Anastasia caught him around the legs again. "Me, too."

"Sweetheart," Victoria began. "Gabriel's been awakened in the middle of the night, rescued your dog, and is taking her to the vet—you know how Molly hates the vet—and you'll be in the way. I think you should stay here."

The child raised a pleading countenance to Gabriel. He shifted, glanced at Anastasia and then the floor. His shoulders lifted with a what's-the-use motion.

His gaze meshed with Victoria's. Something indefinable rested deep in those hazel depths. He was asking for her trust, vowing he could do the job. It touched her, deeper than she wanted to acknowledge.

"I'll care for them like they were my own," he said, and reminded her of a young boy asking for his first quest.

Victoria's breath caught, her heart thudding against her ribs, but her voice eluded her.

"Please, Mama. Molly hurts so bad."

Tearing her gaze from Gabriel's, Victoria took a deep breath and nodded. "Go get dressed and grab a jacket."

Anastasia yippeed down the hall.

Turning back to Gabriel, Victoria touched his hand. He grasped her fingers in a warm, steady embrace. "I never doubted your concern for either of them. Not for a moment. I'm glad you were here tonight."

Gabriel stood stock-still for an unsteady moment. He nodded once. "Me, too."

He carried Molly into the garage and settled her in the car. "My lot in life seems to be toting females," he grumbled.

Victoria bit her lip over a smile. "That's because you're so good at it."

An arrogant, fully male grin smeared across his face. "You think so?"

He was totally incorrigible, completely exasperating, and wholly wonderful. But with that male ego, she wouldn't tell him. Life with Gabriel was spirited enough.

After settling Molly in the backseat, he tucked a blanket around Anastasia's legs. Before ducking behind the wheel, he glared at Victoria, who hovered in the doorway. "Get off that ankle."

She gave him a knowing smile. "As soon as you leave."

"We'll be fine," he soothed.

"I know." But will I, Gabriel? Will I?

SIX

Gabe raised a cup of his strongest coffee to his lips and tipped his chair back on two legs. Molly, her muzzle streaked with patches of purple medicine, dozed on her rug.

Muttering under her breath, Victoria hobbled into the room. A dark scowl marred the smooth perfection of her face.

"What's up?" he asked.

She poured a cup of hot water and reached for the tea ball. "Jillian," she sighed. "Her birthday's in two days, and Bruce promised to be here for it." One side of her mouth lifted in a smile of self-deprecation. "She just got word he won't be here, and it's not a pretty sight."

"Didn't you talk to her?"

Her gray eyes twinkled under arched ebony brows. "Of course, but I'm her mother. I can't possibly know a thing."

"In other words, a fat lot of good you did."

Victoria choked out a chuckle. "You have such a way with words, Gabriel."

God, he loved the way his name rolled off her tongue and through her soft lips. He was grateful for last night's storm, even though Molly had been injured. The ruckus had kept him busy, given him something to keep his overactive mind off Victoria, the nearness of their bedrooms, her sweet acceptance of his kiss.

And her response.

God knew what might happen if he had much time alone with her. An explosion. Like megatons of dynamite. Like unstable yet potent nitroglycerin.

He shouldn't have kissed her. He would've died if he hadn't. If close proximity over the past ten days had strained his resolve and weakened his emotional distance, the kiss had shattered it to hell.

With a small push—or maybe tiny tug—he could have Victoria the way he wanted her. Hot, wild, and greedy for more of him.

But it wouldn't stop there. It would be more than sating a flash of lust. Much more. One touch, one taste, would lead to another, and if he made love to her? Desire shimmied through him, coupled with an image. Victoria, naked, writhing, and focused on one thing. Him. And he on her.

And then what?

Time for a reality check, bub. You're going to bust her brother. Rein it in, man. The lady is strictly hands off.

Her attraction wasn't the only problem. He liked her kids. Hell, he even liked her damned dog. But he was there under false pretenses, living a lie when she'd entrusted her children to him. Not even he was louse enough to take more.

Watching her prepare a cup of hot tea made his gut tighten. And they were in the kitchen. Imagine what seeing her in—or better yet, out of—those filmy under-garments would do.

Gabe shot up and out of the chair. Victoria slanted him a glance full of gentle confusion. Judas H. Priest! If he didn't get away, he wouldn't be responsible for his next move.

Marching across the linoleum, he yanked the door to the garage open.

"Gabriel." Victoria's voice held a wealth of unsuppressed mirth. And damn, but it could stop him in his tracks.

"What?" he barked without turning around.

"Who stepped on your toes and got away with it?"

He angled a black look her way. If she only knew. She'd put him out of sorts and gotten away with it. Only she affected his anatomy in an area that had nothing to do with his toes. "I'll be outside," he grumped. "Maybe I can talk to Jill. Otherwise she'll be hell to live with."

"That'll make two of you," Victoria called to his retreating back.

"Damned women," Gabe muttered, and stalked to the pool. Jill sprawled on a chair, an air of supreme indignation radiating from her.

The prepubescent sulks, he thought with disgust. And leave it to a teen to inflict her ricocheting mood swings on an unsuspecting bystander. Jill, in particular and in most ways, was harder than most to ignore, with an uncanny flair for making the mundane into melodrama. But under those flaming hormones, she was okay.

A bright postcard dangled between her fingers. Her foot jiggled in apparent irritation, and she blew a puff of air up to her unruly bangs, which fell right back into her eyes.

"What's up?" Gabe nodded at the postcard. He was

as put out with her uncle for staying away as she was.
Maybe more.

Jill cast him a baleful look, rolled her eyes, and remained silent. Too bad he couldn't explain how much
he agreed with her. He wanted Hunter under lock and
key. ASAP.

Every day drew Gabe further into the family circle,
closer to Victoria. Too damn close. The scary part was
how easily he'd stopped fighting it. He didn't know
how or why. Playing Victoria's right-hand man had a
crazy effect on him.

Each day wove more silken threads that bound him
tighter to the Devereauxs. Each day would make the
leaving tougher.

He needed to bust Hunter, cuff him, and drag his
miserable hide back to Parrish. Soon. Before he did
something extraordinarily stupid.

Like tumble to bed with Victoria Devereaux.

Jill's jaw jutted out at a stubbornly familiar angle.
The postcard still dangled, her foot still jiggled, and
she still blew at her unruly bangs. He pulled up an
adjacent chair and straddled it.

"Okay," he said, knowing there was no other way
out. "Let's have it. What's the problem?"

Jill sighed. "I don't have a problem."

"Yeah, right. And I'm the king of Siam." Gabe
stared directly into a carbon copy of Victoria's big, gray
eyes. "I don't know a lot of pretty child-psychology
communication, so spit it out, huh?"

She glared at him, and for a moment Gabe wondered
if she'd storm off. The glare was short-lived. Her face
fell, and she tossed the postcard on the table. "Uncle
Bruce won't be back here until next week. Happy birthday to me."

Gabe picked up the note with more nonchalance than

he felt. Bruce Hunter had a bold, arrogant scrawl, but hardly a way with words. "Sorry, can't make it after all. In the Big "O" next week. See you then."

What a heartfelt note. Gabe could've choked the insufferable SOB, but settled instead for adding Jill's hurt to the reasons he'd make Hunter's life miserable.

Looking more child than teen, Jill scrubbed at her eyes, another doleful sigh slipping through her lips. Oh, yeah; Hunter would get his, Gabe promised himself. But good.

"Hey, babe. I'm sorry. Really," he said, surprising himself at the truth behind the words. "But moping around isn't gonna change anything except make you, me, and everybody else miserable."

He patted her shoulder, offering an awkward masculine comfort. "I'll even cook up a special dinner in your honor. All your favorites."

"All in my honor?" Jill straightened, and offered him a weak but interested smile. "Really?"

He made an invisible cross over his heart. "You betcha. Birthdays should be the greatest day of the year. Especially when you enter your teens."

Jill's smile faltered, and she slumped back. "But Uncle Bruce always makes things so . . . fun."

Gabe could just bet! Feigning indignant shock and a gigantic heart attack, he coaxed a muffled giggle out of Jill. "And I can't?"

Springing out of the chair, Jill hugged Gabe quickly, impulsively. "Thanks."

He squeezed her back. "For what?"

She pulled back and smiled at him. "For talking, making time for me."

"I think your mother tried before I did."

Jill looked shocked. "So?"

"So she could've done the same thing. Probably a whole lot better. She knows you."

"Yeah," she said with a slow nod. "I guess so, but—"

"I know, I know. She embarrasses you just by breathing. Must be the way it is with mothers and daughters."

She wrinkled her nose at him. "You're pretty smart—for a nanny. Thanks again."

Gabe swallowed hard and accepted the truth—it got easier each time—and reluctantly hollowed out another corner of his heart for this preteen dynamo. "Sure, kid. Now," he said, scanning around the backyard, "I'm on cleanup detail. Then I'm building man's best friend a new house."

"Can I help?"

"The cool teenager wants to do manual labor?" he asked. Her impish grin was contagious. "Your hands may regret it."

"No problem." Enthusiastic delight lit her face.

Gabe ruffled her unruly bangs. "Okay. Go tell your mom we're off to the lumberyard."

"I get to pick out lumber. Awesome!"

So far, so good, Gabe thought. This way he'd be away from Victoria all day long. How he'd make it through the night was an altogether different problem.

"What're they doin'?" Anastasia asked.

Victoria, the latest glitz-and-glamour best seller under one arm, a tall, dewy glass of iced tea in the other, followed the line of her daughter's dimpled finger. Jill, who under the best circumstances eschewed household chores, not to mention yard work, with something close to horror, was stacking boards and beams in a pile across the lawn. Michael was raptly absorbing instructions from his mentor and striving to carry them out.

A steady *thwack, thwack, thwack* resonanted through the quiet afternoon air. Each solid flick of Gabriel's wrist sent sharp nails skidding out of the old wood of the doghouse. "Looks like Molly gets a new house," Victoria commented.

"She's my dog," Anastasia pouted.

"Why don't you tell them that?" Victoria urged with a nod toward Jillian and Gabriel working side by side. The sight warmed Victoria with a comfortable glow.

Anastasia marched across the lawn to explain bluntly, "Molly's *my* dog. I wanna help, too."

Gabriel dipped down on one knee and cupped the child's nape in his palm. "Want to be my assistant and hand me the things I need to put her new pen together?"

Anastasia looked unconvinced. "Me 'n Molly don't like fences."

"You sure?" he asked. "She told me she loves them."

Two tiny black brows scowled in disbelief. "Uh-uh."

Gabe crossed his heart. "Sure did. Told me fences and doghouses make her feel loved and protected."

"Uh-uh."

Gabe scooped her off her feet and into the air. "Oh? You're not the only one that dog talks to, you know."

Anastasia giggled. Victoria knew that in her child's open mind, all doubts were washed away and everything was right with the world. The cozy scene looked like a family, sounded like a family, and felt like a family.

In the deep recesses of her mind, Victoria didn't mind. She only thought she'd given up the dream. Unconsciously she'd carried around a longing for more zip, more spark, more warmth, than she'd found in her marriage.

The midday heat and the short night converged, covering Victoria in a comfortable haze. Gabriel's low, rumbling baritone meshed with her children's enthusiastic laughter. They'd grown comfortable with one another in a short period of time. If she hadn't known better, she'd have thought the nanny needed the children as much as the kids needed him. As much as she needed him?

Her brows furrowed, but the late afternoon sun erased the worried lines with warm, soothing fingers. A damp nose followed by silky fur nudged under her dangling hand. Cracking one eye open, Victoria stroked Molly's thick neck. The injured animal sat stoically and watched the activity in the backyard, then glanced up at Victoria with liquid amber eyes.

Without a backward glance, the dog trotted up to Gabriel. He bent down, crooned something Victoria couldn't hear, and scratched Molly behind the ears.

"Et tu, Brute?" Victoria whispered. The picture was almost complete. Dog, man, children. It seemed so right. Why was she fighting it? And him? She drifted off to sleep, unable to come up with one good reason.

"Mama! Mama!"

Victoria bolted upright, jarred from a particularly sensual dream about a particularly sensual nanny.

Anastasia barreled across the lawn, her ponytail flying in the wake. "Come see our doghouse. Me 'n Molly love it." Bubbling with exuberance, she yanked her mother's hand. "Come on!"

Victoria allowed her daughter to lead her to the work area. Hunched over the small dwelling, Gabriel hammered shingles on the roof. He was stripped to the waist, his bare torso glistening in the late afternoon sun. Underlying muscles rippled and bunched, and her fascination grew with each movement.

Her husband had never been physical, not in work or play. To him, being a good provider was synonymous with being a good husband and father. It was she who'd wanted more, needed so much more than he had to give.

Gabriel's shoulders and back moved with grace and rhythm, intriguing her and beckoning a touch, a caress, a taste. A sheen of healthy perspiration slicked over his skin, glimmering in the sun. His hair hung loose. Dark brown tendrils clung together, plastered to his neck, held out of his eyes by a twisted red bandana.

Michael, also bare-chested, worked by his side. Gabriel had slung his T-shirt atop the new wire fence around the pen. Flapping in the breeze next to it, slung in miniature hero worship, hung Michael's.

Completely captivated, unable to tear her gaze away, she realized this was what she'd always wanted. Camaraderie, companionship, and love. And Gabriel had given them, combined with a strong, masculine role model. The last of her reservations slid away, and Victoria's heart swelled. "It's lovely, darling," she said to Anastasia. "Did you help?"

"Yeah. Michael hammered nails an' stuff. Huh, Gabe?"

"You bet, darlin'," he said.

"Watch this, Mum." Michael pulled out a nail and handed it to Gabriel. "Ready?"

A wide, sexy grin slashed out. "Any time you are."

Victoria wondered where all the oxygen had gone. She couldn't seem to draw enough into her lungs to breathe or think straight. Her heart spun in her chest.

The condition was directly proportional to Gabriel's nearness, and she didn't even mind. "Seems like you're a jack-of-all-trades," she said with a quick smile, and tangled her gaze with his.

Gabe's lively comeback died on his lips. Victoria's big, gray eyes twinkled with an air of sexy amusement and, if he wasn't mistaken, admiration. Gone was the thin veneer of question and suspicion. In its place was acceptance, and—

"A-a-agh! Hit the nail, not my fingers."

"You moved!" Michael said.

"You missed."

"Did not."

Gabe couldn't miss the mournful tone of voice, the quivering lip, the tears of disappointment and failure welling up in the child's eyes. Hunkering down beside him, Gabe flexed index finger and thumb. "You're right. I moved. I, er, had my mind on other things." Like your mother's fathomless eyes, the softness of her laugh, and a kiss that shouldn't have been. "Try it again. Okay?"

"You gonna blame me if I miss?" Michael wondered.

"You going to miss?" he countered with good humor. "I've only got two thumbs, so this is your last shot."

The boy giggled in a way that captured Gabe's heart. Hell, if he'd fallen for Anastasia the first time he saw her, he'd fallen for Michael at first boyish laugh. Somehow plans had gone completely awry. "Sorry, kid. I shouldn't blame you for my mistake."

"Okay," Michael said, and grabbed the hammer. "Ready?"

Gabe glanced at Victoria, who bit her lip as though holding laughter at bay. Damn, was there anything about her he *didn't* like, wasn't attracted to? Even now, his body stiffened in sensual response just at the sight of her. If he ever touched her passionately, intimately, he was a goner. A blown-to-the-wind-and-outa-sight goner. He'd have to make sure it didn't happen. For both their sakes. "Okay, kid. Let 'er rip. Just like I showed you."

Michael did. Perfectly.

Gabe couldn't keep the pride out of his voice or his heart. "Super." He hugged the boy in a gesture of spontaneous joy. "All of you," he said, glancing at Jill and Anastasia. "You've done one hell—uh, a great job. Really."

Three young faces beamed with unmistakable pride. The mutual admiration Gabe witnessed in their eyes touched him deeply, filling the emptiness of his heart, the hunger of his soul. "So," he said, grabbing his crumpled white T-shirt and shifting the flow of conversation and thought. "We have ice-cold sodas and a panful of rocky road brownies in the kitchen."

The kids rocketed toward the house, jockeying for first place through the door. Gabe watched them with a fondness that would've scared the hell out of him weeks ago. But now it didn't. The pleasure of their company, their smiles, their—

"You're spoiling them."

Their mother. "Isn't that what nannies are for?"

"No." Victoria smiled up at him. Those soft lips haunted his nights. He'd had one taste of her; the consummate sweetness of her smile taunted him with what might be, and could never be. "Nannies insist on three balanced meals a day, a strict bedtime, and no nonsense, and they don't know the first thing about wielding a hammer and nails, let alone constructing a doghouse."

Without warning, she reached for his right hand and inspected it with thorough scrutiny. "How is it?"

Dumbfounded, and unable to piece together a cohesive sentence, Gabe stared at her. Her skin was sleek, like warm velvet encasing his hand. Was she that soft all over? Inside and out? A sudden, overwhelming urge to bury himself in her feminine warmth, absolve himself in the benediction of her body, shuddered through him.

"Well?"

"Well what?"

She smiled, easily and brilliantly. "How are your fingers, goose? My son delivered a mean whack."

That's nothing compared to the whack his mother delivers. He curled his fingers to pull them back. "It's fine."

She didn't let them go. "You'll have a nasty bruise," she said, stroking along his finger, up the curve of his thumb.

His skin burned where her soft caress trailed the calloused underside of his hand. His fingers clamped around hers in a viselike grip, and he steeled himself not to flinch at her wide, startled eyes and quick intake of breath.

"I'm only going to say this once," he rasped. "I'm not a nice man, Victoria. I'm not soft and sensitive and polite." He drew a shuddering breath. "But I want you like I've never wanted anything or anyone. I want you so badly, I wake up at night shaking with it, and I tread a fine line against it during the day."

She nodded woodenly, not moving, but she wasn't frightened, he realized. Not of him, his words, or his wants.

And she should be. Dammit, she should be!

He jerked her up, flat against him, and let her experience firsthand the hard truth of his statement. Gazing into her honest eyes, drinking in the elegance of her face, the soft breasts pressed against him, he could no more stop himself from tasting her than he could deny a request from her children.

How long had she waited for this? Victoria wondered. For him? If his previous kiss had been the embodiment of gentle teasing, this was an assault with a most deadly enticing weapon.

His lips scorched and seared with breathless intensity, and parted hers. His unrelenting tongue glided along hers, demanding and receiving all the dark, wet secrets of her mouth. Hot, salty, masculine, his taste enticed her, and she slid her free hand along his bare waist and up his damp spine.

A cross between a growl and a shudder trembled through him, and as though he couldn't get enough, he pulled her closer, strained against her. She shifted her hips, wanting more of him. He was like a fire in her blood, his kisses potentially lethal.

He tore his mouth from hers and stared down at her for a long moment with glazed eyes. His fingers dug into her upper arms as he struggled with or against himself. "Damn it, Victoria—"

He dropped his arms abruptly, and she lost her balance. Teetering precariously, she bobbled toward him. With a muttered curse about heaven, hell, and the road in between, Gabriel scooped her up against him and headed toward the house. Intense hazel eyes drilled into her. His jaw clenched at a bone-grinding angle.

Victoria cupped his face in her palm, but he flinched away. So lonely and alone, she thought, and pulled her fingers back.

They stepped through the patio doors, intercepted by Jillian flourishing a small manila envelope. "Mother, there you are! You need to sign something for Uncle Bruce.''

"You guys stay put.'' Gabe deposited Victoria on a sofa in the den and strode to the front door. "I'll check this.''

"What's going on? Who's it from?'' Victoria's husky voice followed him, granting him no respite to cool the flash of desire still throbbing inside.

Suspicion sent Gabe's sixth sense reeling. Hanging on the doorjamb was a slick, smarmy man with beady eyes and a slight stoop. "Who the hell are you?'' Gabe demanded in a knife-quiet voice. "And what company do you work for?''

The man, younger and slightly bigger than Gabe, snapped to attention and sneered. "Who the hell are you?''

Instantly Gabe snaked an arm out, gathering the other man's fancy Lauren shirt into a crumpled ball inside his fist. "I asked you first,'' he snarled.

"Gabriel?'' Victoria called. "What is it?''

Gabe half turned following the sound of her voice. The fraction of a moment granted the other man an edge. An elbow in Gabe's ribs threw him off balance and gave the stranger his freedom. In a heartbeat, Gabe bounded onto the porch in hot pursuit. Tires squealed. Gravel spit and spun. A late-model sapphire blue Lotus with dark-tinted windows sped off.

Gabe cursed and slammed the door. "Jill?'' he hollered.

"Yeah?''

He crossed into the den and paced in front of the empty fireplace. "Who's the package for?''

Jill shrugged. "Uncle Bruce. Sent by special courier, too.''

"I thought it was *from* him,'' Victoria said.

Jill turned the package over and frowned. "I don't know. There's no return address, but it looks like Uncle Bruce's writing."

"How odd," Victoria said. "Why would he send himself a package here?"

Good question, Gabe thought, glancing for any untoward reaction from either female. Why?

"Well, heavens, if we don't know who it's from, put it on the library table. Bruce can get it when he comes."

Jill shrugged as if to say, *no big deal.* "Whatever."

Gabe stalked back to the long window by the front door and eased the curtain aside. He didn't know who or what or why, but one thing he did know. Hunter had added to his list of sins. That dude was no courier, not a legitimate one, at any rate.

Something was sure as hell going on, but what? And why?

Why would her wonderful brother have some slimeball deliver a package to his sister's address, knowing she had no one to protect her? Was he getting desperate? Or was there more to Bruce Hunter than merely industrial espionage?

The answer lay in the package. Gabe would check it out tonight, after the ruckus died down and everyone was asleep. Then he'd get a few answers.

SEVEN

Victoria pulled back the white Battenberg lace comforter. Here she was, tumbling into bed, totally exhausted, and Gabriel was still downstairs cleaning!

Jillian's birthday had come and gone in high style. Gabriel had amazed everyone with a blue-frosted bundt cake. He'd simulated a pool with blue color, a diving board with candies and a stick of gum, an umbrella with pretzels and an orange slice, all for the enjoyment of some tiny teddy bear cookies.

The passage of her oldest child into adolescence was completed in high style. Along with the cake were candles, presents, and a resounding chorus of "Happy Birthday." The new teen rewarded her nanny with a teary-eyed hug and a heartfelt sigh of "Thanks."

Gabriel had been pleasant but distracted. The twinkle in his eyes was extinguished, replaced by a preoccupied vacancy. He'd said and done the right things, but all as if by rote. Victoria had thought he was happy. Certainly nothing had indicated otherwise. Was he growing restless already? Preparing to leave soon? Something was bothering him, she thought. But what?

After their confrontation on the patio, she was in no state of dress to confront him. He'd left no doubt as to what he wanted. He wanted her.

How simple. Simpler yet, she wanted him, and that just wouldn't do. The wrapper slid from her fingers to the floor. Tomorrow when she was fully dressed and mentally alert, they could discuss what troubled him.

Where the hell was that damned package?

Gabe stormed into the garage—the last place on his list to comb through. Hunter's unassuming envelope had disappeared shortly after arrival, and Gabe cursed himself an idiot for not grabbing it immediately. Then Jill's party put things on hold for a day.

A real nanny might not notice the small package, let alone its disappearance. The Devereauxs certainly hadn't paid it much attention. So far he was the only one concerned.

He'd scoured the house from rafters to foundation last night and come up with zip. This morning wasn't faring much better. Scanning the well-organized shelves, he lifted each box and bottle, peering over, under, and around each one.

Nothing.

He tunneled an impatient hand through his hair. Although he was loath to involve the kids, he'd spent extra time with them, probed and questioned each one about the missing package.

Nothing.

The munchkins didn't know a thing. There was a look, a cast in the eyes of an active liar. He'd seen it before, repeatedly, and the Devereaux kids didn't have it.

That left only one other person who might know

where it was. Gabe didn't want to consider Victoria, but he was out of options. She had to know something.

He ran a hand under her car's bumper and behind the grille. Popping the hood, he checked the air filter and a dozen different areas where contraband could be hidden.

Nothing.

"Damn!" The lone word summed up his frustration from his fruitless search as well as his reluctance to suspect Victoria.

She didn't have it in her to be a party to illegal skulduggery. Did she? Good Lord, could she have fooled him so completely?

He'd avoided her, drowned himself in a flurry of housecleaning. It provided a dual outlet to find the missing envelope and work off his burgeoning frustration. Victoria'd become an indecent obsession personally and professionally.

How long could he live with her and not touch her? How long could he catch her seductive scent and retain his sanity? Cleaning let him work until his fingers were stiff and his back creaked. The work was less than stimulating, but it allowed him to fall into an exhausted, dreamless sleep. He didn't want any leftover energy. Idle time with Victoria in the house only increased his hunger.

He needed to keep busy until Hunter arrived. Any day.

Any day until Gabe's charade folded like a useless umbrella. He couldn't do anything except tread water and steer clear of her.

A quick reconnaissance of Victoria's car trunk showed no unusual bulges or rips. Slick as a squeaky clean whistle. He slammed it shut with a muffled curse and glared at the door leading to the kitchen.

How could something tangible disappear into thin air? He wasn't one for mysticism or magic. A package he'd seen with his own eyes didn't vanish. Someone had taken it. He needed to find out where she'd hidden it and what it contained. Before Hunter arrived.

Which brought him back to Victoria.

She must have hidden it in the house or on the grounds. He'd driven her everywhere she'd gone, and that was only to see her mother. He made a note to look there, and to stop postponing the inevitable: checking out Victoria.

Turning the doorknob, Gabe ground his teeth together in a fine temper. In addition to his investigation, he had dishes to wash.

Using a carrot stick for leverage, Michael pushed the last half of his lunch from one side of the plate to another. "When's Uncle Bruce gettin' here?"

Gabe's thoughts exactly. Elbow-deep in dishwashing bubbles, he pulled the plug. The water drained with an angry gurgle. He was sick and tired of Hunter's waiting game.

"I don't know, dear," Victoria said in a tone that conveyed it was no big deal. "This isn't like him at all." She lifted a shoulder in a slight shrug. "He's very busy. Maybe something important came up."

Gabe dried his hands on a small terry cloth towel. She was good, he acknowledged. Very good. Watching Victoria lie through her teeth was watching a pro in action. Cool, calm, unflappable. Passing the package off by "special courier" said it contained something big, something the sender didn't want anyone else to see.

"What do you suppose is in the package?" Jill whispered.

"Pictures. What else would a photographer have, dopey?" Michael returned.

"Enough name calling," Victoria corrected without missing a breath.

Jill had enough child in her to stick her tongue out at her brother, Gabe noted with a reluctant smile.

"Maybe it's Madonna, or a hunk on the beach," Jill said.

"Yuck," Michael proclaimed. "If he was lucky, Uncle Bruce got to see the Indianapolis Five Hundred or a baseball game."

What their uncle had gotten was a mess of trouble. Gabe transferred a jug of sun tea to the refrigerator and kicked the door shut. Hunter must've known his package would involve the kids up to their innocent little necks. The hell of it was, they didn't know. Did Victoria? Had her brother fed her a line of garbage to get her compliance?

More than anything, Gabe wanted to believe she'd never willingly do something illegal.

From the moment the manila envelope had arrived, it made the hair on Gabe's neck stand on end. The situation hadn't improved. He couldn't shake the creepy feeling, and he couldn't assess the situation until he knew what was in the package.

But it wasn't here.

"Anastasia, you're awfully quiet," Victoria said, and patted her youngest daughter's hand as it rested on the table. "Is anything wrong?"

"Me 'n Molly're tired."

"Tired?" Victoria asked with a hint of laughter lacing the word. "How can anyone so young be tired?"

Her voice was like fresh honey, thick and rich and sweet. In spite of everything, hearing it made Gabe wonder what it would be like to hear her voice husky with passion, ragged with need in the heat of a sultry night, calling his name.

"Can me 'n Molly go swim?"

"Sounds like you're more bored than tired." Victoria smoothed her daughter's hair and kissed her forehead. "Go on. Have a good time."

Anastasia and Molly followed Jill and Michael out of the kitchen. Victoria's brows pulled together. "Do you think Anastasia's okay? I get the feeling something's not right."

That isn't the half of it, sister. He shrugged. "She's a little mopey, but other than that, she's fine."

"But she's not a mopey child. She's too mellow for that. I just don't know."

Gabe grabbed a dustrag and a can of lemon furniture polish. Though he suspected her, more than ten minutes in Victoria's presence made his blood simmer. She had the uncanny ability to turn him on, over, and inside out with one glance.

She cut him off before he got to the hall. "You're avoiding me."

Bingo, babe! He'd avoided her and the attraction that threatened to pull him under. He'd avoided her to the point of dishpan hands and scrub-maid's knees.

Under the best of circumstances, Gabe was less than patience personified, but living with her had him strung tighter than an overtuned piano wire. "It's Wednesday," he pointed out—brilliantly, he hoped. "And I have a house to clean, Mrs. Devereaux."

"Victoria," she murmured with a smile. Her voice washed over him in a way that never failed to tighten his loins and send his heart clamoring in his chest. The way her smile affected him was almost criminal. "Call me Victoria."

He recognized his own words being used against

him. Had he rattled her cage as badly as Victoria rattled his?

Victoria had missed him. Having grown used to his company, she missed conferring over small daily matters, missed the coziness of a quiet evening together. Most of all, she'd discovered a hollow pocket in her heart that only Gabriel could fill with his teasing smile, his masculine gruffness, and his head-spinning kisses.

In that moment of 1:09 in the afternoon, she wanted nothing more than the touch of his lips, the stroke of his tongue, the earthy taste of him, and so much more. Gabriel Sanders had an eerie way of making her believe in fairy tales.

Gripping the furniture polish until his knuckles turned white, he didn't seem unaffected, either. He turned to leave. Unwilling to relinquish his presence, she reached toward him. Like the man, his arm was strong, warm, and resilient. The thought of those hands on her skin brought a ragged shiver. "Something's bothering you."

"No big deal." Lounging a broad shoulder against the refrigerator, he stared at her. "It's no concern of yours."

"It is if it affects my children," she argued, suddenly on the defensive and not knowing why.

"It doesn't." A crooked smile flashed. "They're great kids, by the way." His smile faded, and he shoved away from the appliance. He stalked to the front foyer to spray and polish an already highly glossed mahogany table with a vengeance.

Victoria hobbled behind. "By the way, have you seen the package that came for my brother?"

His busy hand halted abruptly. "Why?" he growled.

She shrugged. "Because I can't find it anywhere. It's almost as though it disappeared."

"I have no idea." He tossed the dustrag on the sofa

table and faced her with arms akimbo. "I didn't take it."

"You?" His statement was so absurd, she laughed. "I thought since you've cleaned so often and so thoroughly these past days, you might've run across it. I'm not accusing you. You're my nanny. I trust you implicitly."

"Victoria." A deep rush of exhaled breath said he was a man on the edge. Of what, she didn't know.

Gabe plunked the polish and the dustrag on the gleaming mahogany and glared at her. She tied him in knots. He wanted to believe her guilty. He needed to. It was the only way he'd leave her alone. No guilty party had so point-blank bewildered him. He'd handled vehement denials, crocodile tears, and pathetic lies, but never a teasing confrontation like this.

Framing her face in his palms, he tilted her head toward him. Plumbing the depths of her eyes, he discovered everything he'd searched for. Openness, beauty, and guileless trust. "Don't trust anyone implicitly. Not even me."

True to her nature, she shook her head at him and smiled. It pierced him to the bottom of his cynical soul. "I have to. Every moment of every day I entrust my most precious treasure to you. My children."

As though his thumb had a will of its own, it skimmed the curve of her lower lip. "Ah, dammit," he whispered, and lowered his head.

It was wrong, he told himself. She shouldn't let him kiss her. He'd tried to warn her off, but she hadn't listened. He wanted her with a desire so strong, he could taste it.

Their paths were destined to cross and conflict. Even knowing that, he wanted to make love to her. Dear

God, he wanted to bury himself so deep inside her soft body, he wouldn't know where he ended or she began

But he couldn't. Not even he was that low.

But this—he rubbed open lips against hers—this he couldn't help. He planted tiny, humid kisses on her lips, relishing the softness that was Victoria. Her mouth softened, parted beneath his, and rendered Gabe incapable of further thought.

Her varying textures, seductive heat, and genuine sweetness filled him with blinding fire. Whipping an arm around her back, he hauled her soft curves against his harder, more angular frame.

She came willingly, hands sliding up his back, pulling him nearer, as though she couldn't get close enough. The tip of her tongue touched his in a gentle, tenuous foray, and the world burst into a frenzy of orange and red, the color and intensity of overwhelming desire. His blood sizzled and simmered; his groin throbbed. He strained toward her, needing more than a touch, wanting more than a taste. He wanted to sear, to brand, to make her his—

"Mama!" Anastasia's plaintive cry rippled through the house.

With a muttered curse, Gabe ripped his mouth from Victoria's and abruptly set her away from him.

"H-here, darling," Victoria called, teetering on her feet. Her voice was throaty, her breathing rough and labored. "What is it?"

Gabe turned away and grasped the table in a death grip. It was all he could do to keep from pulling her back into his arms and finishing what they'd started.

"Just wondered where you are," came the child's reply. "Can I have a popsicle?"

"Sure," Victoria whispered on a shaky sigh. "Sure," she repeated in a stronger voice.

Gabe clenched his fists and stood motionless in the stony silence of the hall. It seemed like an eternity before the soft click of the patio door echoed back to him. Inhaling on a deep breath, he slowly faced Victoria once again. She reached for him. "Don't," he rasped. "Not unless you're prepared to finish the job. Or," he said with a self-deprecating grimace, "explain the consequences to your kids. I still want you. Too damn much. Nothing's changed."

Grabbing the rag and the polish, he stalked away, stopping before he entered the living room. "Look," he said, and spun to face her. "I'm sorry."

Her flushed face and swollen lips tugged at his heart and his sex. He wanted to say more, to soothe or comfort, but he didn't dare get within arm's reach. Shaking his head, he couldn't ignore the regret welling inside. For the first time in six years, he didn't brush the emotion aside. "More sorry than I can say."

He was halfway across the room before he heard her soft reply. "No, you're not," she said. "And neither am I."

The next day dawned the same as the previous seven. Hot, clear, and dry. Victoria sighed, feeling as empty and arid as the midsummer breeze that always seemed to blow.

It was the Fourth of July. A family day. A holiday.

How did Gabriel intend to avoid her today? She refused to do an ounce of work when everyone in America had the day off. The sound of vacuuming filtered up the stairs and into her bedroom.

Make that everyone else in America except Gabriel.

Forevermore, the scent of lemon would be an instant turn on, always reminding her of him, his fingers framing her cheeks, a dynamite kiss. Housecleaning would never be the same again.

She sighed a second time and burrowed weary fingers through her hair, lifting it off her neck. Where was her head? It wouldn't do to have an affair with the nanny, even if he was warm, wonderful, and sexy as all get-out. That reasoning wasn't much, but it was all she had at the moment.

He'd made it abundantly clear he was attracted but unwilling to take the next step. To seek anything further would compromise her hard-won independence, debase her pride. The price was too high.

Shoving her arms into a flowered wrap, she knotted it at the waist and headed downstairs to give the man of the hour, and unfortunately her dreams, a well-earned holiday.

Downstairs, Gabe used his mother's time-tested "rule of seven": Cover each inch of carpet seven times before moving on to the next strip.

The kids were in the pool, the house was clean, the laundry done—a situation any homemaker in America would die for—and he still hadn't a clue about the damned package!

He'd questioned Victoria's involvement all night. She was the only potential suspect. But if she was a black widow, he'd eat Molly's supper. If she wasn't, where was the envelope? His fingers choked the vacuum handle, wishing it were Hunter's scrawny neck.

"Are you trying to grind my carpet into nubs?"

Gabe jumped and flicked the machine off. How had she sneaked up on him? He hadn't heard a thing. Not only were his investigative techniques springing a leak, his reflexes were slipping, too.

All because of the woman before him.

"Well?" she questioned, a twinkle lurking in her eyes.

"A time-tested method of cleaning my mother taught me," he said, and wound up the cord. "I always had the most spotless carpet in four states."

"Even as a teenager?"

He returned her good-humored grin. "Yeah, but you usually couldn't see it for the clothes and sports equipment laying all over it."

"Don't ever tell Jillian," she said, "but my idea of cleaning my room was shoving all the dirty clothes and miscellaneous junk under the bed. I'll have her hide if she tries."

He shared her laugh, enjoying the moment and the woman. "Your secret's safe with me."

Victoria thought most anything would be safe with Gabriel. Her innermost hopes, her daydreams. Even her heart.

A lingering smile faltered. His gaze fell to her lips, hers to his. The electrically charged moment sizzled.

"Ah," she began, quickly gathering her scattered intentions. "You realize today's a holiday."

A lazy smile kicked up the corners of his mouth with languid ease. "Sure."

"Well then." Her nervous fingers twisted behind her back. As usual, he unnerved her, scattered her composure with one sexy glance. "I thought you might want to take the day off. Everyone else in America is," she added in a challenge.

He shook his head. "Nope. Sorry. Nowhere to go. I've sublet my place, so I thought I'd show you Canadians a real birthday blowout."

"Jillian's wasn't enough?"

"Nope. I'm frying chicken; there's potato salad in the fridge, pop in the cooler, and after the fireworks, we'll have homemade ice cream with enough fat and calories to choke a horse. "But," he said, wiggling his brows, "it'll be great."

His sensual lips drew up over straight white teeth, and Victoria's heart almost stopped. "Why, Gabriel, I do believe you're a romantic."

He smiled as though she'd lost her mind, as though nothing were further from the truth. "Why, Victoria, I do believe you're crazy."

She shook her head. "I think not."

"Time's a-wastin', Mrs. Devereaux. Let's get this show on the road."

Stepping in stride with him, hitching every once in a while, she adjusted her gait to his. "You're planning a regular Yankee Doodle day, aren't you?"

"Anything wrong with that?"

"You're not only a romantic, you're the worst kind," she gloated. "Incurable."

"You're nuts."

The burgeoning aroma of fried chicken tempted her palate. "And the fireworks?"

"They're illegal in the city," he commented dryly.

"So is speeding," she argued, rather rationally, considering their close proximity. "But it's done all the time."

"Think you're pretty clever, don't you?" Grabbing her upper arms, he hauled her close. "Just how clever are you? I wonder."

Before she could formulate a reply, he released her. "I'm clever enough to know you better than you think. You may have convinced yourself you're not nice, or gentle, but not me. Not in a million years."

"You don't know what you're talking about," he said, and stalked into the kitchen.

He'd planned the whole day around her family. A

regular old-fashioned Fourth of July picnic and fire-works. What woman could resist the gesture? Not her.

In that moment, she understood. She was hooked on the nanny she'd hired for her children, a man filled with an innate kindness and tenderness he couldn't admit, but showered in full abandon on her children. In return, there was nothing she wouldn't give him. Including her scared-to-love-again heart.

At dusk, Gabe, sated and drowsy, lay back on a large quilt on the lawn and closed his eyes. A moment later, a small body landed smack dab in the middle of his abdomen. "Whoa, sugar," he said, catching Anastasia up over his head. "There's a mountain of fried chicken in there."

"There's a whole flock of chickens in there," she said, and giggled merrily.

He swung her down beside him. "And there's a whole bunch in here, too." He leaned over and tickled her tummy.

"There's some merit to her claim," Victoria commented from the opposite end of the quilt. "I thought only teenage boys ate like bottomless pits."

"No," he said slowly, drinking in the sparkling gray eyes, the softness of her encompassing gaze. "Sometimes hungry men do, too."

She laughed, a husky rasp in the twilight. "You can't be hungry, Gabriel."

"Oh, yeah?" he breathed, and sent her a knowing look that melted her insides. He could ignite the ocean. "I'm ravenous."

"Then let's dig in to your highly touted strawberry ice cream. My arm was almost wrenched out of its socket from all that turning."

It wouldn't touch the hunger he'd referred to, and

Victoria knew it. She was baiting him, teasing, tormenting, and loving every minute. Gabe set Anastasia aside and stalked toward the house. "Five dishes of homemade ice cream coming right up."

Victoria was playing with fire.

"Is it time for the fireworks yet?" Michael sighed as if he'd waited his entire life.

Victoria scanned the sky, noting the darkness inching in. "I think so, but check with Yankee Doodle over there."

"Very funny," Gabriel returned. "Okay, guys, we'll start with sparklers."

The dog didn't like the bright, spitting spangles. Shuddering, she slinked off under a bush.

"Molly don't like fireworks," Anastasia announced.

"She sure doesn't," Gabe said, pulling the dog close. He patted and caressed the animal until her trembling stopped.

The kids hovered around, each flinging a comforting arm around the family pet. "She can sit with me," Victoria said. "You three enjoy the show."

Gabe lit the remaining cascades, showers, and rockets to appreciative gasps and murmurs. In the light of the last flare, the evening gloom paled in comparison to the three glum expressions facing him.

Even Jill's crestfallen face was a mirror of her siblings'. "Is it over?"

Gabe didn't have the heart to tell her yes. Besides, he wasn't ready to call it a night, either. He'd had a good time. Too good. They were all going to fall, and hard. Him included. Even so, he couldn't let the night end.

It all felt too damn good. Genial, comfortable, and

loving. Like a family. Hell! How had he waded in so deep? Why didn't he want to get out?

Turning to a smiling Victoria, he battled the urge to reach out and steal a little bit of her warmth. "There's quite a show at Rosenblatt," he said, referring to the annual blowout that followed the local AAA baseball team's holiday double-header.

Her smile would eclipse the rocket's red glare. "Sounds wonderful."

They tucked Molly in the basement, and within fifteen minutes, were all strategically settled on a small hill. Amazing pyrotechnics exploded directly overhead, dancing to patriotic tunes. Anastasia, nestled between Gabe's legs, watched each burst of light and color in total rapture.

Jill lounged against her mother's side. Michael braced folded arms across Gabe's back. A family, Gabe thought. A real cozy cocoon, not too different from a well-worn pair of snug slippers in the winter. Now he knew what he'd been missing, and it wouldn't be easy to give it up.

The kids were silent, almost reverent, during the entire display. Within an hour, the food, the excitement, and the fireworks had taken their toll. They were asleep.

"I'll wake Jill," Victoria said, anticipating his direction before he'd voiced it. "Can you manage the other two?"

"Sure." He roused the younger two with a loving expression that filled Victoria's heart. "What about that ankle?"

She shifted Jill. "No problem. I've adapted to it quite well."

He knew the feeling. Unable to wake Michael, Gabe lifted Anastasia in one arm and the boy in the other.

Both drowsily nuzzled deeper into the hollows of his shoulders.

Gabe swallowed around a lump in his throat. Hell, if this didn't win him first prize for masochist of the year, nothing would.

EIGHT

What made Gabriel tick?

The question continued to plague Victoria. It consumed her as she stared out the large bay window in her second-story bedroom and observed his nightly smoking ritual.

As was his habit, he settled under the large sugar maple west of the pool. His broad back nestled against the broader trunk of the tree. He drew deeply on his cigarette, the spot of incandescent orange glowing hot in the stygian night.

The first quarter moon offered silvered illumination and revealed outward distraction in his motions. A hand dangled off his right knee, tapping in open agitation. With a lift of his muscled wrist, he raised the cigarette to his lips.

If she lived to be a thousand, she'd never forget the gentle way he'd hoisted her two sleeping children in his arms and enfolded them against his solid chest. If the way to a man's heart was through his stomach, the way to Victoria's was through her children.

I'm not a nice man. She leaned her forehead against the glass and drank in his darkened silhouette. Not true. Victoria knew what he couldn't admit.

He was a man of honor. True to his word, he'd never smoked around any of the kids, always waiting until after everyone retired to indulge his habit. He saw himself hard and uncompromising; Victoria saw him steadfast and unwavering.

Don't trust me. How could she not? It hadn't been an active choice, more like a comfortable notion that wrapped around her bit by bit. Each day pulled her closer to him, like the unsuspecting moth to a beckoning flame.

He was a man capable of evoking fierce loyalty, not only in her children but in their family pet. They adored him to the point of worship, and after today, they would be bound even tighter.

The same held true for her whether she wanted to admit it or not. His smoothly muscled arms had wrapped around her children, and his roughly whispered endearments stole not only her heart, but a piece of her soul.

I'm no good for you. What he did to her bordered on instantaneous combustion. He'd stampeded over her defenses and trampled her best intentions.

He wanted her. She wanted him. What could be simpler?

Nothing. Everything.

Closing her eyes, she skimmed her tongue across dry lips. Instantly she remembered his taste, his scent, his touch. If not for the interruptions of her children, she knew what Gabriel's kisses would've led to. She doubted she would've regretted it.

He opened an emotional Pandora's box and rattled her stodgy existence. Order, routine, and organization had been her life for six years. She knew her role and had her part down pat. No surprises, no ambushes.

Until Gabriel.

He stirred up embers long banked and jolted her back to the world of the feeling whether she liked it or not. In so doing, she realized she was scared. Deep-down, toe-curling scared to love again.

Her father, her childhood Prince Charming, had deserted the family when she and Bruce were preteens, leaving her mother to cope financially and emotionally as best she could. Determined her own marriage would last, Victoria stuck it out through eight years and three children. The result had been the same. Her husband had left her for a younger, sexier woman. A few minutes later, he wrapped his car around a telephone pole, and Victoria had maintained the facade of widowhood ever since.

Life had taught her well. Love was frail, fragile, and fleeting. Forever only occurred in fairy tales.

Her gaze flicked back to the broad-shouldered shadow outside. But oh! how she wished it weren't so.

She wanted his sheltering arms around her, his face on the pillow next to her. She longed for forever, and she doubted Gabriel could provide it.

The fiery stub of his cigarette made another crescent voyage through the inky night before he ground it out. Something seemed to occupy his mind. What?

He pushed off the ground and whistled for Molly. Dutifully the dog raced toward him, and was rewarded with a hearty scratch behind the ears. Gabriel straightened and scanned the back of the house, his gaze lingering at Victoria's window.

Her hand flew to her lips. With her bedroom light off, he couldn't see her. Even so, her mouth went dry and her heart slammed into high gear. He never failed to bring her feminine radar to screaming awareness.

Gabriel locked Molly in for the night. Victoria slid into bed, listening for the soft snap of the dead bolt he'd recently installed.

Click. The sound reverberated through the silence.

His soft footfalls on the stairs echoed comfortably through the second floor. She heard him enter and exit each child's room, checking on them before he sought his own bed. Established since the first night he'd been there, the pattern imbued Victoria with a sense of security.

He stopped outside her open door a long, considering moment. Her breath caught; her lungs froze. He moved on.

Victoria rolled onto her back and pressed trembling fingers to her lips. His startling effect on her grew stronger each day, and in the ebony blackness of midnight, she had to admit, it felt a lot like the dreaded state of love.

Strains of "The Wanderer" blended with the steam roiling to the ceiling. Gabe stepped from the shower and yanked a fluffy bath towel off the rack. With a muffled curse regarding his situation, his disposition, and life in general, he swiped at a sliver of mirror and glared at his reflection.

Drawing the towel down the length of his body, Gabe called himself every kind of fool. He was soaking in the Devereauxs' warmth and goodness, milking it for every drop he could.

He was caught like a rat in a trap. Oh, the trap may have heavenly, even silken, bars, but he was every bit a low-down, dirty sneak in this scenario.

Gabe whisked the thirsty terry through the dark

thicket of chest hair as though he could scrub away his sin. A spark flickered up his spine, then quickly scampered down.

Something was in the air. His bones crackled. His skin hummed with barely contained energy. Today would be the day.

He slung the towel around his shoulder and slipped into a fanny-molding pair of black bikini briefs and snug Levi's. His towel-dried hair hugged his neck, clung to his shoulders.

Brown eyebrows pulled together in an elemental frown. Hazel eyes glared back at Gabe from the mirror. In twenty-four hours, he'd be out of here, out of their lives, out of their hearts.

Oh, yeah? They wouldn't have hearts after he got done. Gabe's chin jutted out, and he scrubbed the dark stubble with shaving cream. Those were the breaks, he told the cold, silent man in the mirror. Life wasn't fair, nice, or just.

He regretted what was coming. Didn't that count for something? He needed to settle up with Rick and duck back into the shadowy netherworld of bail bonds and bounty hunters. It hurt too much to live in the light.

Scraping his razor across a jaw that had often been called stubborn as well as square, his hand faltered. The tremor nicked his skin. Blood oozed bright red.

Gabe stared, remembering six years ago, when he was a rookie cop. The call had come from dispatch. His wife, pregnant with their first child, had been in an accident. Dull, dark blood surrounded her. So much. Too much. Hers. The baby's.

"No!" He thought he'd buried it all. The hurt. The pain. Like those who'd forgotten the past, he was condemned to repeat it, only this time with the Devereauxs.

Unsteady strokes finished the job, and Gabe wiped

his smooth cheeks. He placed his razor on the counter and turned to complete what might be his last day. Instead of elation, the only emotion he could muster was dread.

"Sing with me, Gabe." Anastasia offered Gabriel a long wooden spoon to double as a microphone.

"I don't know, short stuff. I'm awfully busy."

"Aw, phooey. You haven't had any time all day. Don't you want us no more?"

Victoria caught the conversation and eased her office door open. She couldn't put her finger on it, but something was out of place today. For one thing, Anastasia never found fault with anything Gabriel did. For another, Gabriel never passed off any request from Anastasia.

His shoulders stooped with a sigh, and he slowly turned to face the child. "Which song?"

"Shoop-shoop!" her daughter called out, bouncing up and down with a wooden spoon for a microphone.

A smile lifted Gabriel's somber lips. "Okay, darlin'."

His full, rich baritone clearly called out the words telling every woman how to discover if she was loved: in his kiss. Victoria took heart. Surely Gabriel felt something for her. He couldn't kiss her with such fire and not feel something.

Anastasia shoop-shooped through the chorus with in-bred do-wop and collapsed against Gabriel in a fit of giggles.

"Hey!" he cried in mock horror. "Where's my backup?"

"I think she's taking five," Victoria said from the door. "For a giggle break."

Gabriel's hearty laugh stopped abruptly. His gaze lingered on her face, her lips, her breasts, before returning to lock with hers. "Sorry. Were we interrupting?"

She clomped her way to the table, and slid into a chair. "I was ready for a break. You two are more interesting than columns of numbers. By the way, you have a lovely voice. Very rich."

"Yeah?" he asked, eyes lighting with a teasing spark.

Pleased with the reaction she'd wrung from him, she smiled. "Mmm. What woman could resist a man who knows all the words to golden oldie love songs?"

"How do you know what lyrics I remember?"

"I wake up to your morning serenades."

Gabriel's mouth dropped open, then snapped shut.

"Well, your voice projects well, and the shower is only across the hall." Images of a wet, naked nanny wearing a decidedly wicked grin stole her breath. "Ever sung professionally?" she rushed on in a move to re-route the conversation.

He barked out a poor semblance of a laugh. "In my business, there's not much call for singing."

Her brows lifted in surprise. "Not even an occasional lullaby?"

"Ah," he stumbled, "sure. But it's been a long time since I've handled babies and stuff."

"Whoever you sing to, I'm sure they love it."

"Me, too," Anastasia complained around a Popsicle.

Victoria wrapped her arms around Anastasia and dropped an affectionate kiss on her smooth forehead. She tilted her head, catching Gabriel's wistful expression, full of longing and something more. Pain.

She didn't know why it would be there, but it was. Perhaps it had something to do with whatever had him so preoccupied last night.

The urge to pull him close and ease his concerns and

obvious worries almost overcame her. To avoid doing exactly that, she sprang out of the chair and headed back to work. "I'll be in my office if you need me."

He needed her more than he could say. He didn't want to. It wasn't healthy to need anyone. It only compounded the pain.

"Let's swim, Gabe."

Nothing would hurt as much as losing his baby. Gazing into Anastasia's round, innocent eyes, he knew betraying this family would come close. "Sorry, sugar. I can't." He swung away. "I've got to get supper started."

"Aw, phooey." She sighed, shrugged, and tossed her wooden spoon in the empty sink.

Let it be, man. Let her go. But he couldn't. She hadn't asked for him to screw up her life, and she sure as hell deserved better. "Wait till I'm done here."

She plodded to the French door, turned, and raised her doleful gaze to him. "Promise?"

At his nod, she said, " 'Kay," and closed the door behind her.

Anastasia wasn't herself, Gabe thought with a frown. Nothing major, but she was lacking her usual spark. Victoria's kids had personality plus. In the future, memories of them would haunt his nights and never be far away during the day. That was the burden of involvement and—dare he admit it?—love.

He loved the kids. Damn! Just what he didn't need.

B-R-R-N-G . . .

Gabe stared at the telephone, every instinct humming.

B-R-R-N-G . . .

Get it, hot shot. This is it.

B-R-R-N-G . . .

"Yeah?" he breathed into the receiver, glancing over

his shoulder to make sure Victoria was safely tucked in her office.

"Uh. Gabe?"

"Thompsen?" His subordinate wasn't exactly the excitement he'd anticipated, but then again, things had run awfully smoothly for the past few weeks. No emergencies. No priority cases. "I thought I said *not* to call me," Gabe all but barked. "What the hell's the problem?"

"Uh. Well . . . that hundred-fifty-thousand-dollar bond you wrote before you left?"

"My cousin," Gabe ground out, not liking the heavy sensation that curled in the pit of his stomach.

"Uh. Well . . . he split right after you went to Omaha, and you said not to bother you. I've been trying to find him. Had a hellacious chase down I-29 last week, but I lost him. Haven't seen hide nor hair of the little monkey till today."

"Where is he now?"

"According to your aunt, holed up at his girlfriend's."

"Then go get him," Gabe said through clenched teeth.

"Can't. I mean sure I can, but the judge refused to extend the bond, and ordered—got that, Sanders? ordered—you, not me, to haul your cousin's butt before the bench by nine o'clock tomorrow morning. I'm telling you, he is one mad mother—"

"I get the picture, Thompsen," Gabe said with deadly quiet. "He wasn't too happy about setting bail in the first place." Gabe sighed. He'd been none too pleased to write it. He'd done it for his aunt, his mother's only sister. She'd begged, pleaded, and put her home up as collateral. But if a capricious judge ordered it, it had to be done. Gabe wasn't throwing away

$150,000 on anybody, related or not. "Give me the address."

Gabe jotted the information down, glancing at Victoria's office door. He'd only be gone a couple hours at best. If he got right back, he'd be ready for Hunter whenever he showed up. Luck had been with him so far, and this latest twist shouldn't be a problem. "Meet you in thirty minutes. Stake it out until I get there, and stay put!"

"You play around in Omaha, and come home for a shakedown and a bust. How come you get all the fun stuff?" Thompsen said with a chuckle.

"Because I'm the boss," Gabe returned. "You'll do well to remember that and get on stakeout. Call me on the car phone if anything changes." He hung up the phone and strode toward his supposed boss's office. "Victoria!"

Glancing up from her work, she blinked and gazed at him through her reading glasses. "Yes? What is it, Gabriel?"

The glasses were plain, nondescript, and made her look sexy as hell. He'd love to see her wearing only those spectacles and a butter-melting grin. Halfway into the room, he stopped. Admit it, Sanders. She's the real reason you're ducking out for a few hours.

Okay, he admitted, he needed some space between them, or rather, his raging libido did. "Something came up," he said, hiking his thumb toward the kitchen. "I've got to go, but I don't have supper started or anything. This shouldn't take too long. Maybe a couple hours."

Her husky chuckle cut off the remainder of his explanation and spiraled through his senses like a hot knife through butter. "I can handle things on this end. I survived by myself for six years; I can handle two hours."

She smiled, her soft, pink lips drawing up over straight white teeth. Gabe's breath caught in his throat. Acting strictly on instinct, he backed up two paces. "Great."

Her smile widened, as if he amused her. "See you later, then."

Once out of her office, he headed for his car at a pace just shy of a run. And it had nothing to do with his bail-jumping cousin.

"Where's Gabe?" Michael asked.

"Yeah," Anastasia chimed in.

"Supper isn't the same without him," Jillian chirped.

Even Molly's amber gaze held a question, Victoria noted. "Something came up that he had to take care of."

"What 'mergency?" Anastasia asked.

"I don't know, dear. I didn't pry." Victoria sent her daughter a pointed look that said, *and you shouldn't either*.

"Aw, nuts." Michael hunched over his supper.

"Don't slouch, sweetheart," Victoria corrected by rote.

"It's awfully quiet, Mother," Jillian commented. "Were we like this before he came?"

"Like what?"

"You know, boring."

"You were," Michael parried. "You were born boring."

"Michael Alexander, that's quite en—"

"Hey, hey, hey, guys!" A masculine voice, definitely not Gabriel's, boomed from the front door. "Can't a guy get a happy hello around here?"

The children stopped, stock-still, and exchanged mutually questioning looks. "Uncle Bruce!" Jillian cried and, dropping any pretext of pending young adulthood, raced down the hall.

"Cowabunga!" Michael agreed, and followed suit.

Anastasia hung back.

"Come on, sweetheart." Victoria held out her hand, and Anastasia clasped it tightly. "Let's go see Uncle Bruce."

"Vic!" he called.

Her smile froze into a tight line. She hated the nickname, and only one person used it within earshot.

Bruce, animated as always, spun around and engulfed her in a bear hug that lifted her off her feet. "Hey, baby sister. Nice to see you. I was just telling my nieces and nephew we're booked at Adventureland for the weekend."

"Wait," Victoria said on a half laugh. "You just got here. Don't you have to recover from jet lag or something?"

"Chill out, Vic." Bruce's smile vanished. "You got a problem here?"

Victoria drew back in his embrace and searched his face, looking for what, she didn't know. "Just motherly concern."

"Good." He hugged her back to him. "Go get your bags packed, kids. We'll leave tonight, be back first thing Monday."

"Bruce . . ."

"Oh, Mother. We haven't gone on holiday in ages," Jillian pleaded.

"Yeah," Michael called in a double-up-on-Mother play. "Not since our weekend in Niagara last year, and that was too sweet. Come on, Mum. Please, please, please?"

She should have expected it. Bruce usually took the children on weekend outings. But today there was something different, something more unsettling than his Tasmanian devil-like arrival. "What about Mother?" she asked quietly.

"You three go up and pack three pairs of shorts and tops, a bathing suit, comfortable tennis shoes, and socks. Go!" Bruce waited until they were up the stairs and down the hall.

Safely out of hearing range, she noted. "I haven't said yes yet, Bruce. And you didn't answer."

"Look, Vic. We both know the score. Ma doesn't know who I am. I could be Walter Cronkite for all she knows. Why should I spend my few days of free time in a depressing nursing home with someone who doesn't even know the year?"

"Because she's your mother," Victoria said.

"You always did have a thing about motherhood, didn't you?" Bruce pecked a kiss on her cheek. "Okay, okay. We'll see her when I get back. I just finished a tough assignment, and I need R and R like nobody's business. Here's our room and the telephone number at the inn."

"You're pretty sure of yourself, brother dear."

"I'm the best uncle they've got."

"You're the only uncle they've got." She hesitated. There was a too bright sparkle in his eyes. And he was jittery, as though he couldn't light in one place too long.

"Well . . ." He tapped his foot in feigned impatience. "Give me one good reason why they shouldn't."

What could she say? That she had an "iffy" feeling about the whole situation? Hardly. The idea barely made sense to her! She had nothing concrete to argue with or against. Outnumbered, or perhaps outwitted, she could only shrug and hope for the best. "Have a good time."

"A-a-w-w right!" Michael and Jillian high-fived their success at the top of the stairs and barreled down.

"Annie-stace." Bruce motioned the child forward. "Come on down."

Anastasia gripped her small bag like a lifeline. Her little-lost-waif stance tugged at Victoria's heart. She questioned the quickness of this weekend visit, but before she could delve into it more thoroughly, Bruce waved Anastasia down the stairs. Molly skulked behind her miniature mistress.

"Still got that mangy moose you call a dog, I see," Bruce said with a snicker, and ushered the child down. "Come on, kiddo. Time's a-wastin'."

Anastasia paused in front of her mother. "Gabe didn't remember to swim with me," she said simply, and was gone before her mother could form a reply.

As she waved good-bye from the porch, an unsettling sense of restlessness filled not only the empty, silent house, but Victoria herself. She couldn't make sense of anything, let alone her feelings. Everything was so jumbled up and confused.

One thing, she did know. Three very important people in her life were acting completely out of character. Gabriel, Bruce, Anastasia. "What's going on around here?" she asked out loud.

Molly's doleful whine was her only answer.

NINE

"Damned idiot!" Gabe passed a lone car cruising at the too slow speed limit. He raced his white Trans Am through the evening gloom, sucking up the miles between Council Bluffs and Victoria's house as if they were premium unleaded. Damn! What a waste of time.

Gabe's fingers eased over the knot on his temple, and he winced. A bitch of a headache throbbed in his skull, radiating out in all directions. The run-in with his cousin had turned into a new law for Murphy.

Like most red-blooded Americans, his ill-informed relative labored under the delusion that a private home was safe refuge from the police. That was true. But not for Gabe. Not as a bounty hunter.

He needed nothing more than an identification card to cross state lines, break in doors, or whatever it took to bring the fugitive to justice. Reasonable force got damned unreasonable at times, he noted with a scowl. Rolling around on the floor trying to handcuff a frantic dude who'd turned into all arms and legs had its drawbacks.

Lighting a cigarette, he drew in a deep breath and cursed the tenderness in his side. Nothing broken or cracked. Nothing taped or splinted. Bruised ribs, according to the emergency room doctor, who'd been none too sympathetic for Gabe's taste.

Two hours had passed into four, then five. His idiot cousin, the fight, the booking and jailing, Thompsen's infernal clucking over his injuries, all combined to trip Gabe up and slow him down. He was more than ready to head home.

The cigarette halted halfway between the ashtray and his lips. When had Victoria's place become *home*? He glared at the stick of menthol as if it had sprouted wings.

God, he was getting maudlin! Slushy, mushy, and heart-drunk. Disgusted, Gabe threw his smoke out the open window and concentrated on the road. The starless night was heavy, ripe with electrical sparks on the distant horizon.

Humidity hung in the air, the breeze blowing damply against Gabe's cheeks. His broad hand raked through his hair.

Bright shards of lightning spit in the distance. Tension twisted in his belly. He'd been so sure something big had been in the works today. With a muttered expletive, he dismissed the thought and pulled into the drive. The dark house loomed silently in the night. A thread of disappointment knifed through him. You've got no reason, Sanders. It's not your house; she's not your woman; they're not your kids.

When it came to Victoria and the kids, he had no right to feel anything, but he did. He couldn't stop the desire, the passion, she stirred in him. He wanted her jet black hair spilled across his white pillow. He wanted to peel her barely there nightgown off her slender body and slide those slinky straps down her arms. He wanted Victoria until his palms itched and his body ached.

Ah, Victoria. You tie me in knots.

He not only wanted Victoria, he admired her. Strong as steel, yet soft as kid gloves. Motherly, yet feminine. Giving, loving, and stubborn as hell.

He couldn't hold out much longer against either his desire or her allure. Too keyed up to sleep, he needed to reevaluate the situation. Everything would look better after a hot shower and a cold beer.

He unlocked the door and pushed it open. What he wouldn't give to have her waiting up for him, concerned about his absence, maybe even worried. But she wasn't. Hell, he thought with a rumbling sigh. A guy could dream, couldn't he?

Victoria paced the patio and scowled at the burgeoning darkness. Where was he?

A couple of hours, he'd said. A couple of hours had come, a couple of hours had gone, and Gabriel still wasn't home. Where was he?

Bruce and the children had called four hours ago to tell her they'd arrived safely. Gabriel hadn't called. Something was wrong. She was sure of it. Maybe there'd been an accident? Who knew better than she what a deadly combination an automobile and bad luck made? Where was he?

Lifting her hair off her neck, she turned and paced back toward the door. This was ridiculous. He could take care of himself. He'd told her as much. More important, why did she care if he couldn't?

Victoria's legs stilled, and a cold dose of reality rooted her to the spot. She loved him. It was that simple, and that complicated.

How the fates must be laughing. The woman too

smart to fall in love, who'd ordered her life to avoid that complication, had been bushwhacked. What was it her mother used to say? *The faster you run away from something, the faster it catches up with you.*

Love had certainly caught up to her. She loved Gabriel with every fiber of her being. Did she have the courage to act on that fact? Seize the moment? Or would she hang back and not take a chance? The price of love was high, but the price of fear was higher.

A shaft of white pierced the obsidian darkness. She stared at the strip of light for a moment before realizing its origin: the kitchen.

Bent at the waist, head almost buried in the refrigerator, was Gabriel. Relief flooded Victoria. A small smile crept out.

He was home and looking so sexy, her heart wrenched. Simultaneous urges to fling herself into his arms in sweet welcome and strangle the life out of him for worrying her vied for supremacy. Like steel to magnet, the splinter of illumination drew her to the open door and whatever lay beyond.

Gabe grabbed a cold beer and twisted the cap off. Bracing an arm on the refrigerator door, he lifted the brown bottle to his lips and pulled a healthy swallow.

Movement shimmied at the corner of his eye and caught his attention. The beer hesitated just shy of his lower lip as he focused on the shimmering iridescence. It approached, luminous in the darkness, drawing closer, gaining substance and shape—and oh, what a shape! Straight out of his fantasies.

He was barefoot and naked from the waist up, Victoria noted with approval. His unbuttoned jeans revealed the pale skin of his hips and a dark pocket of coarse hair, leaving little to her overactive imagination.

She drew closer. The glower on his face gave her

second thoughts, and she hesitated. "I—I was worried about you."

In the scant light, heat flashed in his eyes, but it was quickly erased. "Yeah?" he drawled, and arrogantly downed another long, deep swallow. "In case you forgot, I'm a big boy. I can take care of myself."

How could she forget such an obvious fact? "Even big boys get hurt."

Lounging on the open appliance door, he lazily lifted the beer once more. His gaze traced the outline of her body with a thoroughness that stole her breath. "You don't know the half of it, lady."

His comment excited and disconcerted her. Out of her element and in shaky territory, she grabbed at a mundane subject for protection. "Want something to eat?"

An almost smile hovered around his lips, and Victoria's heart jumped into high gear. He wasn't half as fierce as he'd have her—or the world in general—believe. Seizing that small fact as truth, she stepped toward him.

"Nothing here looks half as good as you," he growled.

Victoria stopped where she stood. A long dry spell had come and gone since a man had honestly expressed to her that she was desirable. The admission sounded good and felt better. She stepped toward him seeking more.

"Stay where you are," he barked. "I'm not in the mood for games."

"I'm not playing games." She wasn't. She was stone-cold serious.

"The hell you're not," Gabriel said in a gritty voice full of male heat. He ran the back of his knuckles, bottle still in hand, along the vee of her white satin camisole. "Are you a lady in bed, too, Victoria?" Eyes narrowed to slits, he leaned toward her. "How long do those manners last before you sweat and pant like the rest of us?"

His humid breath tickled her ear. Warm roughness from his hair-dusted skin blazed a fiery trail, cooled by the smooth bottle. He skimmed the slopes of her breasts, down her breastbone to the edge of the fabric covering her and a millimeter farther. She shivered at the delicious textures and gauged the sincerity of the question by the smoldering depths of his eyes.

Suction, a feeling like quicksand, pulled at her belly. A dark dampness gathered at the apex of her thighs. "Do you really want to know?" she whispered, unable to stop the words, unwilling to deny herself. "Are you ready to put up or shut up?"

Gabe's breath rushed out in a heavy lump, but that was nothing compared to the knot Victoria created below the waist. He'd tried everything, verbal warnings, physical bluffs, but rather than running away, she moved closer. Dangerously close. So close, his own resistance had been chipped away. A man could only take so much, dammit! He slammed the bottle against the top of the refrigerator.

She moved, and her white satin wrapper whisked across his chest, teased his hypersensitive skin, taunted him with everything she was, everything he wanted. "Victoria," he rasped, "I'm not kidding."

Her breath fanned over his lips a moment before her mouth reached for his. "Neither am I."

Gabe was lost, swirling off in a vortex of hot passion and unquenchable desire. His arms snaked around her, hauled her several inches off the floor, and plastered her against his chest. If she wanted to play with fire, fine. She'd been stoking this one since the moment they'd met. A volcano wasn't any hotter than he was.

Victoria gave in to the moment, the sensations, the man. How long had she wanted this? Him? Ages. Eons. Too many long, lonely hours. Now she had him, and he was more wonderful than she'd ever imagined.

Need spiraled quick and fast. He twisted his hand in her hair and tipped her head farther back. She grabbed his broad shoulders to steady herself.

"Tell me to go to hell," he growled. "Tell me to stop—"

"Stop," she murmured through a delightful haze. "Stop playing." Her fingers raked through his thick hair, climbing from scalp to silken ends. "Stop this torment. . . ."

A groan, half plea, half prayer, escaped his throat before he clamped his mouth on hers. God, he'd tried. He'd avoided her until he ached. He grabbed at his last straw before sanity slipped completely. "The kids."

Victoria nibbled along his lips, cheeks, and jaw, stopping only to whisper in his ear and push him over the edge. "Gone overnight. Be back Sunday."

Alone. They were completely and totally alone. Victoria leaned into him. Sensation descended on Gabe, enveloping him. The cool satin of Victoria's clothing contrasted directly with his feverish skin. The faint scent of her perfume coiled around him, beckoned him. Before he could think further, Victoria's teeth raked along his earlobe, and clusters of ragged explosions rocked him. Heat radiated from her, devoured him. Desire—raw, primitive, and too long denied—burst between them.

Fine, tiny tremors shook Victoria. Whether they came from Gabriel or herself, she didn't know, didn't care. Her frenzied hands roamed over his smoothly curved biceps and sturdy shoulders, digging into the solid muscle with a frenzy of pent-up need. She couldn't get close enough, couldn't taste enough, couldn't touch enough.

Gabe's palms slid to her waist. Somewhere in the back of his mind, his rusty conscience clanged in alarm. This is wrong. He was with her under false pretenses. She didn't know. She wouldn't want this if she did.

Her inquisitive fingers roamed the wide pelt of curly dark hair on his chest. Her touch pulled a low moan from him. "Gabriel?" she asked in a throaty voice that shredded his rapidly dwindling control.

"Helluva time for a chat," he murmured, covering her neck with openmouthed kisses. Untying her wrapper, he greedily peeled it over her shoulders and down her arms. It fell in a silken pool around her ankles. "I want you. To see you. Touch you, everywhere."

Victoria struggled to hold on to a thin thread of self-control, blindly pulling him closer, scattering myriad kisses along his shoulders and chest. "I—"

"What?" With a wicked grin, he hooked his fingers under the wisp of lace that passed for her panties and skimmed them down her soft legs. "What do you want? Do you want me to kiss you slowly, deeply, thoroughly? Do you want my mouth all over that gorgeous body? Should we drag this out, Victoria? Take it slow and easy and drive you over the edge, or do you want it hard and hot and fast? Tell me."

In response, her soft hands skated down his spine, under his Levi's to cup his buttocks. "You," she said in a husky voice that robbed him of thought and speech. "I want you. In every way."

"You got it, babe." Her ragged murmurs of acceptance drove him senseless. Echoes of recrimination died in the face of some minor facts. He was here; she was here. He wanted her; she wanted him. Of that he had no doubt.

Ribbon-thin chemise straps drooping onto her slim upper arms snapped under his frenzied hands. With a sharp curse, he shoved the short gown to her waist, freeing her breasts to his hungry gaze. His eyes seduced her, teased with unspoken promises and made her feel altogether a woman. She knew the magnetic effect he had on her, but she wasn't prepared for the wildness he evoked, the primitive, untamed passion he sparked.

"Perfect . . . you are so perfect," he said, and lifted her to his mouth. He feasted at each breast in turn. Lips, teeth, and tongue tasted, scraped, laved, each in turn, worshiping as though at a perfect altar.

Victoria's head fell back. A low moan rippled out. He was a wizard, conjuring up forbidden, delicious sensations. Her bones liquified. Her stomach fluttered to her throat. Electric chills raced up her spine, down her arms. She was freezing and overheated at the same time. A heavy throbbing beat between her thighs. Gabriel created the hunger, fanned the fire, and only he could put out the flame.

He lowered her down his front and pressed her naked hips intimately against him. Denim rasped against her softness. Desperate desire, unknown before this man, consumed her. Pleasure detonated in her loins.

Gabriel grunted with increasing impatience. With an efficient motion, he pushed the jeans down his lean hips and kicked them off. With no further preliminaries, he lifted her, hesitating one last time, shaking with the effort it cost him. "You're sure?"

"If I'm not?" she teased with a kittenish grin, and nipped his lower lip.

He ducked his head to her shoulder and shuddered,

his strong arms quaking with the restraint. "I won't walk for a week, but I'll live."

Laughing softly, Victoria framed his jaw between her palms and kissed him thoroughly. "You talk too much."

With a deep breath, he lowered her onto himself, filling her wet tightness until he was completely sheathed. "My God."

Victoria arched like a tightly strung bow. He'd been right. What a more than perfect fit they made. Leaning her upper back against the side of the refrigerator, she wrapped her good leg around his lean waist, and her braced one around his thigh. His muscled shoulders bunched and flexed, and she reveled in his power and strength, the erotic beauty of him, of this, of them.

Gabriel moved inside her, long, slow thrusts that carried her higher and higher. The rhythm of her thoughts ebbed and flowed with the rhythm of their bodies. God—she'd wanted—all her life—to feel this right—this complete—this hot—nothing had come close—ever—with anyone.

Her long legs tightened around him, and Gabe flew higher and higher. Hot dreams and torrid fantasies paled in comparison to the flesh-and-blood woman. Her name tripped off his lips like a prayer.

Her wet heat stoked him higher, hotter, raging out of control. The flame would never be extinguished. But God, what a way to go!

Victoria whispered his name. He fused his mouth to hers, his tongue and his body plunging into her fast and hot and hard. She met and matched him taste for taste, touch for touch, but knowing once would never be enough. In the end, insatiable need burst into a shuddering, soaring climax. Victoria held him close as though to protect him and herself. From what, she couldn't imagine.

Later in the darkness, it didn't matter. Smoothing her fingers along his vertebrae, down the small of his back, and lower still, she smiled in thorough contentment. "Mmm. There's a lot to be said for a comfortable bed."

"Especially if you're in it." He growled the words against her neck, nipping the soft skin, then laving the pinkish area with his tongue. His hands skated along her curves, investigating hollows and hills, peaks and valleys. Especially the peaks.

"A-a-h . . . Gabriel."

"Is that a good a-a-h or a bad a-a-h?"

Her breath hissed through her teeth. "Dear God, where did you learn to do that?"

His fingers delved and probed, rubbed and skimmed. Hard, then soft. Giving, then demanding. "Where did I learn what?"

"A-a-h . . . that . . ."

"There's that 'a-a-h' word again. You didn't say, is it good or bad?"

A strangled gurgle, somewhere between a laugh and a moan, erupted from her throat. "A-a-h, Gabriel. It's good. So good." After a silent moment, she writhed beneath him and sighed. "And you know it."

"Nah." A cheshire cat grin caught at his lips. "Tell me about it." He kissed her. Long. Languid. Lingering. "Better yet, show me."

She did.

"I'll give you three hours to stop that."

Victoria's seeking hand stilled, hovering over a flat male nipple. "Only three hours?"

He sent her a mock scowl, and pressed her hand back against his chest. "Okay, three days."

She insinuated a smooth leg between his. "Better."

Gabe groaned. "For who?"

"Whom."

"Whom what?"

Her laughter, full and infectious, seeped into his hungry heart. Her arms encircled him, and her forehead touched his chest. "Oh, Gabriel. You're wonderful."

He brought her hand back to his chest. She wouldn't say that if she knew why you're here. He stifled the ugly thought immediately. He wouldn't allow anything to intrude, to spoil the joy of being in her arms. It would be a sacrilege. Regrets would come, and he'd live with them. Later. "I've been called a lot of things in my day; wonderful wasn't one of them."

"A real tough guy, huh?" She smiled and outlined the intriguing tornado-shaped hair covering his torso with the tip of a slow, damp finger. "How interesting."

Her finger dipped lower, and he tensed. "Not half as interesting as your fingers."

A low, husky sound of amusement trickled through Victoria's lips. "Glad you like them."

"Like them?" he wheezed. "I adore them."

"I adore you."

God, did she really mean it? Was it possible? "Don't, Victoria. I—"

Stemming a potential self-derogatory statement, Victoria kissed him with an intensity she didn't recognize as her own. Kissed him until her toes curled and the aching emptiness throbbed anew. "Don't say anything bad about yourself. I know you in ways you don't."

"Really?" His smirk was tolerant, patronizing, and infinitely masculine. Resting his head on his stacked hands, he nestled into the pillows. No one was going to deny him tonight. He humored her, playing along. "What do you adore?"

Brushing her lips across his, she accepted the challenge. "Your mouth," she breathed. "Your lips, your tongue, and the delicious things they do," she said, and excited herself with the memory.

He lifted his head to kiss her, but she angled away and ran her tongue along his jaw. "Your stubborn jaw. It's always stuck out at such an arrogant angle."

He twisted toward her, but she pushed him back into the pillows. "You asked for this," she whispered, her lips scraping against his ear, her breasts brushing his bare shoulder. "So listen real good, tough guy."

Dragging her open mouth along his chest, she circled one nipple with the point of her tongue. His sharp intake of breath was her reward, and she smiled. Dozens of heated, humid kisses dotted his chest, and his heart hammered under her ear. She laved his second nipple with the same loving attention she had the first, sucking and nipping lightly.

"I'm listening," he grated. "But I don't hear much."

Writhing her way up his firm, muscled torso, she braced herself above him, dropping light kisses on his forehead, eyelids, nose, and cheeks. "Try again."

Her tongue contoured his ear while her small hand wreaked havoc with the thin arrow of silky, dark hair that trailed from his ribs to his groin. Her fingers wrapped around his hard, velvety length, stroking him until he thought he'd die. Raising onto one shoulder, he gasped for a well-earned breath. "Victoria!"

She kissed him again, long and slow, weaving her tongue into the rich textures of his mouth. His arms shook; she pushed him down and straddled his hips. Lowering herself by slow millimeters onto his thick, throbbing shaft, she leaned forward and whispered, "Get it yet, tough guy? Everything about you is wonderful. The way you look at my children, the way you treat my dog. I adore every inch of you—"

His husky groan met her shaky, tattered breath. "Some inches better than others."

"They're all the same."

"Not hardly, lady." His rough palms framed her hips, and he thrust up. She rotated against him, throwing her head back with a gasp. "Not hardly," he growled.

Once again, his long, smooth strokes drove her to the brink of infinity and beyond. She tipped her head and sighed softly. Hands at her waist, he pulled her forward, fastening his mouth on her breast with delicious, delightful, totally carnal wetness.

Pleasure shuddered through her, and a small cry escaped her lips.

"That's it," he purred. "You talk your way. I'll talk mine. Listen, Victoria. What do you hear?"

"Gabriel," she breathed against his lips.

His groan of fulfillment mated with her violent trembling in an ending so sweet, so long, so drawn-out, he forgot everything but the woman in his arms.

Collapsing on his love-slick chest, Victoria wasn't capable of anything except lying there. His heart thudded heavily under her hand, slowly returning to a more normal cadence. She trembled again and kissed his chest. "Can you feel it?"

Gabe sighed with resignation and twirled his fingers in her dark, silky hair. She'd dragged him this far back to the world of the living; he couldn't be less than honest. "Yeah, babe. I feel it."

Funny thing was, he did. He felt everything. Every beat of her heart, every sigh from her soul, and damn his selfish hide, it felt great. More than great. It felt like heaven.

TEN

Sunlight beat against Victoria's eyelids in a red haze. Consciousness seeped into her brain by slow degrees. The rhythmic puffs of soft male breathing ruffled the hair on top of her head. Her cheek pressed against a warm, muscled wall that rose and fell in lazy undulations.

Contentment, a cat-in-the-cream satiation, rooted her in place. She nuzzled against him, one hand skating down his bare hip, the inside of her good foot skimming up his hair-roughened calf.

Instantly her shoulders were caught in a viselike grip. Before she could blink, Victoria was flipped onto her back and pushed into the mattress. "Gabriel!" she squeaked.

His dark brows merged in a fierce scowl, as though he were reorienting himself in unfamiliar surroundings. "Victoria?"

"Good morning to you, too." Slipping her arms around his back, she smoothed down to the softer skin of his lower back and lifted up to kiss him.

"Sorry," he said with a rueful grin. He dipped his head to playfully nip her neck, raking his teeth against her skin. "I'm not used to waking up with anyone."

She smiled. "I'm glad."

"The rug rats spent the night somewhere?"

"Glad to see it's all coming back," she said dryly.

He nudged his hips against her thigh. "That's not all that's coming back."

A fluffy pillow trimmed in white lace bounced off his forehead. "You're incorrigible."

Easing against the headboard, he pulled her up against him. "What happened to 'wonderful' and 'I adore you'?"

Victoria sniffed and anchored the sheet under her arms. "Such a selective memory."

"Not selective," he said, and dropped a kiss on the tip of her nose. "I've had so many hot, steamy fantasies about you, that I couldn't adjust to reality."

"Fantasies?" Intrigued and pleased, she grinned. "Really? Since when?"

"Since I met you."

A shiver rippled through her. "Oh."

"Yeah. Oh." He drew her across his chest, holding her lips centimeters from his. "Lady, what you do to me . . ."

"What?"

A grin tweaked his lips. "How much time do we have?"

"Mmm," she sighed. "All weekend. Bruce and the kids will be back Sunday evening. They start Bible school Monday."

His body went rigid. "Bruce?" he asked softly. "As in your brother?"

His reaction surprised her. His withdrawal confused

her, and she eased reflexively to her side of the bed. "He took them to Adventureland."

"Your brother." Gabriel sat up and raked strands of dark hair back from his forehead. "Took the kids."

A sudden coolness, a vulnerability she'd never experienced around Gabriel, crept over her, and she tugged the sheet covering her breasts higher. Victoria frowned. Why did Gabriel care? What did it matter? "Is something wrong?"

"Do you trust him that much?"

"He's my brother." Of course she trusted him. She'd always trusted him. Never mind that he was acting strange. She pushed her concerns aside. "Bruce always takes them somewhere for a few days when he comes to town. It gives me a break, free time to myself."

"Why didn't you tell me this last night?" His accusatory tone set Victoria on edge.

She stared at the man in her bed. Where was the tender tough guy who'd made love to her all night, the man who'd touched her guarded heart? This Gabriel was unrecognizable, a cool stranger. "Informing you of my children's whereabouts wasn't high on my list of priorities last evening." She shot him a knowing look. "Conversation wasn't a big item for you, either, if I recall."

A corner of his mouth hiked up in a semismile that turned her insides to mush. "Touché," he said. "It wasn't. I was much too consumed with your many—" he traced his finger across the sheet covering her breasts, then slipped under the percale to stroke her flesh "—obvious charms."

"You have an odd way of showing it." A frown lined her forehead. She sighed at the deft maneuver of his hands and struggled to stand her ground. "Your bedroom manners stink."

His larcenous grin flowered into a full-fledged smile. "What a tacky thing to tell your lover, Victoria."

She rolled the word "lover" around in her mind. "Is that what we are? Lovers?"

The question seemed to catch him off guard, and for a moment he struggled with the answer. "Isn't that enough?" he asked huskily.

No, not nearly enough. She wanted to erase the pain in his eyes, wanted to wake beside him every morning. *Play it by ear,* an inner voice prompted. *Take it slow.* "Whatever you can give is enough."

Capturing her fingers, he tugged until she was pressed along his length from breast to knee. "You deserve more than I can give you. So much more."

He pulled back and looked down at their bare bodies melded together. In the bright morning light, she shifted uncomfortably. "Don't."

A chuckle rumbled through his powerful chest. "Don't what? Don't look at you? After what we did last night? All night? Sweetheart, I know every inch of you by taste and touch and smell." One hand cupped her chin, the other smoothed her long, dark hair off her face. "I know my way around you blindfolded. And you're beautiful."

"A body that's carried and nursed three children is anything but beautiful."

"Who fed you that one?"

He met her gaze head on, held it with such intensity, she could hardly breathe. She glared back, hating to admit her shortcomings out loud. "The only other man I've slept with," she snapped.

"Your dear, departed husband?" he asked with a

cynical twist of his lips. "I hate to speak ill of the dead, but he was obviously blind."

"No," she said with a sigh. "It's the truth. My breasts droop, my belly's lined with tiny scars, and, as Arthur used to say, 'it just doesn't feel the same.' My God," she muttered, and turned on her side, "I can't believe I'm saying this."

Gabe gathered her back to him. "I'm glad you did." Pinned under his heavier weight, she could barely move, which was exactly what Gabe wanted. Reports were misleading, and he'd misread Interpol's stark data. He'd interpreted a happy marriage, but this information shed a different light. Where there was a put-down, there was a weak man. And where there was a weak man, there was a vulnerable woman. He hated that Victoria had had to put up with it, no matter how long ago. "That was one man's opinion. Doesn't mine count?"

He didn't want her believing those lies. He wanted to erase them, erase the self-doubt he saw on her face. He insinuated his hips between her legs, the friction of bare skin on bare skin heating his blood again.

"Gabriel—"

His mouth moved over her ear, abrading the soft, sensitive shell. Her nipples tightened under his palms. "What?" he whispered against her temple.

"Please . . ." The rest of her sentence dribbled out in a throaty gasp as his teeth raked over an already taut nipple. His tongue burned a trail down her side, sliding into the indentation of her waist. He nipped at the curve and slipped his hands to meet at the base of her spine.

"Please what?" he panted, wondering with his last working brain cell how far into masochism he really was. His arms shook, and he held her close to still the tremors.

"Love me. . . ."

His hands closed over her derriere and squeezed lightly. With a low, hungry growl, he pulled her toward him. "Oh, darlin', yes."

Once again, he filled her body with his. Once again, he knew it would never be enough. If he lived a thousand years, spent a thousand nights like the one past, it would never be enough. Victoria got to him in a way no one ever had, ever could. He kissed her, evoking the hot, wet action he sought where their bodies were joined. "You," he said, looking her square in the eye, "are beautiful. That's the God's truth."

Tears filled her silver-gray eyes and clawed at his heart. "Aw, hell, Victoria. I didn't mean to make you cry."

She smiled, and one lone tear escaped its dam and trailed down her ivory cheek. He caught it with his tongue. "You poor men," she said with a light laugh. "Tears aren't always sad. Sometimes they're happy."

"And these are happy?"

"Very happy," she insisted, and kissed him until he thought he'd burst.

"Bet I know something that'll make us both happy."

"Really?" she asked, playing his teasing game very well, stretching out the desire bubbling between them to the snapping point. "Whatever could that be?"

He withdrew, almost completely leaving her. Her hand on his lower back stopped him. "I don't think that's it."

He surged forward. "How 'bout this?"

Her eyes fluttered shut. "Mmm. How 'bout you do that again. And again. And again."

Gabe luxuriated in Victoria. The warm wetness of her body surrounding his, the slick satin of her skin pressed to his, the sweet nectar of her mouth. He wanted to chase the old memories away. He wanted to bring her happiness, even if it was for only a short time.

In the cooling afterglow, regrets flooded Gabe. Victoria slept peacefully in his arms. She was beautiful in every way, and he shouldn't have touched her. He knew the type. When she gave her body, her heart was already there.

He had no business seducing the lady of the house, no matter how willing and warm and wonderful she was. Rules were rules. Yet how could he have refused? Where Victoria was concerned, he didn't think, only reacted. She filled his senses until he could see nothing else. She was his fatal flaw, a point of vulnerability.

The key to his salvation would be if she saw through her brother. A mighty big if. He was a fool to even think it, but try as he might, he couldn't dim the fledgling hope. Only time would tell. With a heavy sigh, he nestled his cheek against Victoria's hair. He didn't have much time left.

"Your brunch is served, madam." Gabriel flourished a large silver serving tray laden with toasted English muffins, several jellies, scrambled eggs, a pitcher of orange juice, and a single pink rosebud. His open white cotton shirt flapped at his waist in the perpetual breeze. Ducking his head and shoulder under the umbrella's shade, he laid his offerings on the table.

With his bare chest mostly exposed, his back to the sunlight, and his feet planted firmly apart, he looked like a buccaneer from a bygone era.

Unable to ignore the dainty flower, Victoria lifted it to her nose and inhaled its sweet fragrance. "Thank you."

"You got it all wrong, darlin'. I should be thanking you," he said with a theatrical leer.

Victoria couldn't drop the smile that had been her constant companion since they'd gotten out of bed. She couldn't dismiss the honeyed glow that swizzled through her every time she looked at him. And she couldn't tamp down the delicious heaviness that tightened her stomach each time he gave her his I'll-have-you-for-dessert grin.

Only one tiny doubt lingered on the fringes of her mind. What about Monday, Tuesday . . . and all the days after?

She loved him; of that, she had no doubt. He wanted her with a passion that left her breathless. Of that, she had less doubt. But what about him? Could he be more than an intermittent lover?

Victoria shivered in the bright sunlight. She wouldn't ruin the here and now with worries about tomorrow. The future would take care of itself. Whatever happened, happened. The "what ifs" and "why fors" would come later.

"Much more of this, and I'll be spoiled completely rotten," she said, twirling the flower beneath her nose. Its sweet scent mingled with his spicy after shave.

"What are nannies for?" he countered with a knowing look and a smile that would make time stand still.

With a laugh, Victoria laid down the rose and took up her plate. "I believe nannies are for children, not mothers."

"Spoilsport," he chided with good humor.

Gabriel grabbed an empty glass and the pitcher of juice. Victoria watched his every motion, a symphony of fluidity and efficient movement. He was relaxed and sated, and his usual reserve had vanished. She'd never seen him so open or at ease, and discovered she adored this well-hidden side.

He held out her glass, and while she reached for it, Gabriel filled his own. It was then she noticed his scuffed knuckles, bruised and swollen. She gasped and grabbed his empty hand. "What happened?"

The hand that had stroked her so gently during the night, so ravishingly that morning, curled into a fist. "Nothing."

Not to be put off, she anchored her fingers around his wrist. "Don't be absurd. It's very much something."

"Let it go," he mumbled.

She glanced up, but his other hand, well hidden under the table, betrayed nothing. He was only gone once, and the marks had to have come from then. "Yesterday's emergency?"

"Yeah, so what?"

He looked caught, trapped, and somehow guilty. He wasn't going to volunteer a thing, and their relationship was too new for her to push. Clasping his fist between her hands, she kissed the scraped skin.

Breath hissed through Gabriel's teeth. "What are you doing?"

"Kissing it to make it better." She blessed each joint with her mouth and tongue. "Don't shut me out. I want to know the good and the bad. Talk to me."

Gabe's lungs stopped, trapping his breath inside his body. Could she really take the bad with the good? Or was it too much to hope for? Her moist heat might've kissed his battered hand, but it was his heart she soothed and made better. What could he offer in return?

"Let's just say the other guy looks a helluva lot worse, and he's real sorry he hit me. Okay?" A crooked grin slid across his face.

"Did he apologize?" she pressed.

Oh, you beautiful, innocent doll! "No, the police locked his butt in jail."

"Jail? That's why you were so late—and I was worried sick. Why didn't you let me know? Didn't they give you a phone call? Isn't it against your rights?" She fired the questions one after another, not allowing him time to breathe, let alone answer. Finally he covered her mouth with his hand.

"I appreciate the concern," he told her, his voice gruff with emotion he'd wanted to deny but couldn't. "But I didn't get booked, the other guy did. I was late because I had to stop by the hospital."

"Why the hospital?"

He sighed and laced his fingers through hers. "I thought I had a cracked rib."

Her gaze darted to his open shirt. "Ribs, too?"

Leaning back, Gabe pulled the cotton aside to reveal an ugly discoloration on his side. She hadn't noticed it earlier, but then, she hadn't been looking for anything untoward. "Satisfied?" he asked.

"The outside will heal," she said. A profound sadness flitted across her eyes. Her hand smoothed through his long hair, down his cheek. "What about the inside? That's the hurt I'd kiss and make better if I could."

The statement was so on target and unexpected, it caught Gabe off guard one of the few times in his life. Speech escaped him, and he could only stare at this beautiful, intuitive, very special woman. The woman he'd betray in a few short days. He wished he had the strength to pull away, to leave her alone, but he couldn't.

Damn him! He wasn't that strong.

Her soft palm traced the angle of his jaw, and he turned to place a quick kiss at its center. "You're really something, you know that?"

Leaning forward, she touched her lips to his. "So are you, tough guy. So are you."

Yeah, but wait'll you find out what that something is.

Much later that evening, Victoria lay next to him under her canopied bed, the steady thud, thud, thud of his heart under her ear. The rhythm soothed her, lulled her into a complacent lassitude. Tonight his lovemaking had taken on a different cadence, one tinged with urgency. He'd demanded her all, and in return, gave more than he took. In the end, he'd seared himself onto her soul.

Her fingers swirled and circled invisible, nonsensical patterns on his chest. His well-satisfied murmur completed her contentment. For a long while she lay beside him, her body entangled with his.

"I get the impression your marriage wasn't exactly great," Gabriel said as though it were the most natural thing in the world.

Surprised, she jerked her head up. "What?"

"I was thinking about our conversation this morning. You seemed pretty upset to think I'd shut you out. That, and your remark last night, led me to one conclusion."

Nestling her cheek against his warm bare flesh, she pecked a kiss on his chest. "It doesn't matter anymore."

And it didn't. She didn't care what her husband had thought. Funny how easily she'd shed that burden. In the face of Gabriel's care and concern, his smoldering anger at a man who'd carelessly insulted her body and femininity, she realized only one opinion mattered. Gabriel's. "No marriage is ever what we think it will be."

The regular breathing pattern stopped. "No," he said rather thoughtfully. "It sure isn't."

"My husband got bored after eight years," she told him, arching her leg against the hand he slid down the back of her thigh. "I was seven months pregnant with Anastasia when he left. Just walked into the house, said he was tired of me and everything else, and wanted out. So he packed his things, took his sporty new car, and sped down the road."

Gabriel cursed softly and explicitly.

"He only got a mile and a half from home when he actually ran into a telephone pole." Gabriel's hand squeezed the back of her neck in mute sympathy. "The girlfriend he'd left us for showed up at the cemetery after everyone else had gone."

Gabriel's arms tightened around her, and he dropped a lingering kiss on the top of her head. "Talk about the end of innocence."

She nodded, her cheek skimming his warm skin. The words tripped out, tumbling one over another until they became a torrent. "I felt sorry for her, but I hated her. She was physical evidence of my failings. I kept trying to figure out what I'd done wrong, but he hadn't said, and I . . ." Victoria frowned and sighed. "I didn't have a clue. Still don't."

"Well, I do," Gabriel said vehemently. "He was a weak, stupid bastard, Victoria. I'm sorry, but he was. You were too strong, too smart, and too much a woman for that wimp."

She pressed a kiss to his throat. "Thank you, but I wasn't the person then that I am now. Maybe he was right. I probably was boring and not sexy enough."

Gabriel snorted. Strong hands caught her under the arms and lifted her to face him in the soft lamplight. "You're sexy as hell, lady, and anything but boring."

"You're prejudiced."

"You damn betcha." He kissed her, curling one

hand around her neck to plunge into her hair and anchor her mouth against his. The kiss deepened, growing hotter and more carnal with every swirl and thrust of his tongue until they were both panting. "You didn't do anything wrong. The man was a bloody idiot if he couldn't appreciate you. Especially when you were pregnant with his child."

Her fingers roamed aimlessly over his torso, down his side. "You like children, don't you, Gabriel?"

"Yeah."

"You're very good with mine. It's a shame you don't have a family of your own."

"Yeah," came his husky reply. A long time passed, and Victoria might have thought he'd fallen asleep except for his broad hand skating up and down her spine. Finally he shifted and tucked her against his side.

His thumb skidded along her lower lip. "I was married—"

"You never told me—" He laid a long finger on her lips.

"It was six years ago. It didn't have anything to do with us until now." Rolling back against the headboard, he stared over her head at the wide, blank ceiling. "We were married about a year when Diane got pregnant. I wanted to wait a little longer, but . . ." he shrugged negligently. "Anyway, the baby was due in six weeks. There was an accident. Drunk driver smashed into her head on."

His hand sliced through the air. "One fell swoop. Boom! No wife, no family, no nothing."

He fell silent. The silence drew Victoria's gaze. The pain she'd only glimpsed before etched onto his face full force. Brushing her fingers across his brow, she longed to ease his burden. Not knowing how, she let him talk.

"Actually, that isn't quite true," he said softly. "Diane was dead on arrival, but they took the baby C-section. That tiny little thing was a miracle. A real fighter." He shook his head as though the memory were almost too much. "A little girl." His voice fell to a hush Victoria could barely hear. "Only lived eight weeks."

"Oh, Gabriel. How awful." Victoria clasped his hand, tension coiling through his muscles as though he fought to accept the pain. "The doctors couldn't say why. Just one of life's nasty curves. Autopsy said lung problems, but . . . I'd gotten to hold her that last day. And rock her. At least I had that."

"Oh, God." Victoria's blood ran cold, and she wrapped her arms around his waist and hugged him close. Of all the heartaches in the world, losing a child had to top the list, but losing a baby? Those sweet, soft bundles of joy? It was horrible, unimaginable. When a child died, parental dreams died, too. "I'm so very sorry. I don't know what to say that isn't trite and inadequate." She punctuated her words with a light kiss of consolation. "I have no right—"

"You have every right. It's the one honest thing I can give you, and God, I wish it was more." He hugged her tightly, and drew in a deep, shuddering breath.

Her arms cradled him close, and she held him for a long, quiet time. His fingers sifted repeatedly, almost thoughtfully, through her hair.

"No wonder women are always yammering and pushing men to talk," he said. "Confession is good for the soul."

"I'm glad I was here."

"I'd have had a tough time doing what we just did without you," he said, and kissed her hard and quick.

"But I'm glad you were here, too." His admission bound him tighter, more implicitly, to Victoria than before. The first was physical; this was emotional.

He should be breaking away, not tying himself closer, but he couldn't seem to do it. Without his permission, she'd carved herself into the deepest caverns of his heart, burrowed in for the duration. There wasn't one damn thing he could do about it. And he really didn't care.

Sunday came and went too quickly for Victoria. Torn, she wanted a reunion with her children and brother, but their presence would mean an end to the openness of her relationship with Gabriel. For a while. Until they had time to sort things out.

Every tick of the clock was against her. And him. Gabriel seemed to sense it, too. Caresses and touches were varied and numerous. So were the kisses of varying length and strength. After a lingering supper, she curled up on the sofa next to Gabriel and decided it was her favorite place to be.

"We've got to talk about this," she said.

"A womanly dissection of things?" he asked, eyes brimming with mirth.

"What happened to 'confession is good for the soul'?"

His rakish grin jolted her heart. "Not necessarily on a daily basis," he said, and reeled her forward for a particularly knee-melting kiss.

"Gabriel—"

"God, I love the way you say my name." His hand inched up her turquoise tank top. "I love the way you feel." His teeth nipped her ear at the same time his hands cupped her breasts.

His thumbs found her nipples, rubbing back and

forth, up and down, until she was panting so hard, she didn't have breath for his kiss.

"God, Victoria," he groaned.

A sharp *thump, thump* sounded a moment before the front door burst open and Anastasia's voice rippled inside. "Mama? Gabe?"

Victoria immediately sprang to attention and straightened her clothes.

"Judas H. Priest!" Gabriel mumbled. "That kid's got lousy timing."

Victoria stood and tucked in her top. "How do I look?" she asked Gabriel.

"Good enough to eat," he drawled. "Go on ahead. It'll take me longer to get presentable."

Victoria laughed and hobbled to the foyer. Anastasia wrestled with pulling her suitcase into the house. "Mama! Help me. Where have you been?"

Grabbing the suitcase, Victoria lifted it and the child into the house. Michael, Bruce, and Jillian trekked up the walk. "I was busy, dear. How was Adventureland?"

In a moment she was inundated with childishly exhuberant hugs and kisses. A trio of voices spoke at once in a cacophony of excitement and explanation. "Wait a minute. I can't hear anybody."

"Okay, guys. What did we decide?" Bruce asked. Her children fell silent. "Before we regale your mother with war stories, take your stuff upstairs and unpack."

"Aw, phooey!"

"What a drag!"

"That's hard!"

"Go, go, go," Bruce insisted, and watched them troop up the stairs. His intent gaze combed over Victoria's face until she shifted in the embarrassed silence.

"How were they?" she asked.

"Triple delights as always," he returned. "So, where's the marvelous Marvin Poppins I've heard about for the last three days?"

"That would be me." Gabriel's icy voice knifed through any formalities. "The name is Sanders. Gabriel Sanders."

Neither man extended a hand. Both stared with determined intensity, and Victoria wondered at the masculine face-off. "Gabriel, my brother, Bruce Hunter."

Her brother and her nanny glared, neither flinching or moving away. She touched Gabriel's broad hand with familiar intimacy. "Be a dear and help the children unpack."

"Isn't that common fare for a nanny?" Bruce all but sneered. "Why should he be a 'dear' for doing it?"

She grabbed Bruce's arm in a no-nonsense grip. "We'll be on the patio when you're through," she called after Gabriel. "Join us, won't you?"

"Since when do servants mingle with the family?" Bruce demanded.

"Since the older brother acts like an ass," she returned, and shoved him toward the door.

ELEVEN

Upstairs, Anastasia wrapped her arms around Gabe's legs and hugged him. "I missed you."

A warm emotion he didn't readily identify drizzled through him, and he smiled. "I missed you, too, short stuff."

"I dreamed you left." She clasped him tighter. "You won't leave me, will you?"

Her voice held an odd quality, decidedly ominous. Still, her words tugged at his heart. Bending down on one knee, he pulled her close. "I can't promise that, sweetheart. No one can."

Her bedraggled ponytail sat at a woefully lopsided angle. He couldn't resist an affectionate tug. "Hey, what gives? No self-respecting pony would wear a tail this far off kilter."

Anastasia cuddled into his chest and giggled. "Jillian doesn't do as good as you."

"Didn't your uncle help?" The moment he said it, Gabe could've kicked himself. On sight, he hadn't liked Bruce Hunter. The man was too slick, too sharp. But his prejudices about the sleazy jerk of an uncle shouldn't color Anastasia's outlook.

She drew back, staring at him with a wariness Gabe had never noticed before. "I don't want him to do it."

A curious attitude for a young child, he thought. "Why?"

Her fragile shoulder lifted a fraction. "Just 'cuz I don't. I like you to do it."

"And I like to do it, but that doesn't mean I'm the only one who can." Grabbing a hanger, he handed it to Anastasia and pointed to the open overnight bag.

Small fingers closed around the plastic-coated metal. "I love you, Gabe."

Nothing had prepared him for the certainty and suddenness of her statement. His body stopped functioning. Brain shut down, lungs quit, heart stopped. Of all Victoria's children, his most special relationship existed with Anastasia. Partly because of Anastasia herself. She was honest, open, and loving as only a young child could be. Too soon the world would teach her otherwise. Gabe had fallen for Victoria's children hard and fallen early. Not realizing the preciousness of his find, he'd fought against it, but no more. His hand skirted down to cup her head. "And I love you."

"Forever and forever?" she asked, her wide, innocent eyes shining up at him.

"Forever and forever." He whispered his answer, trying to ignore the gigantic lump in his throat. Sudden heat burned his eyes, and he blinked several times to clear his field of vision. "I've got to check on Mike and Jill," he said huskily. "I'll see you later."

Gabe oversaw the older kids' unpacking. Zigzagging from room to room, he listened with half an ear to their hearty exclamations about the Raging River and Falling Star rides. Concentration escaped him. Anastasia's declaration haunted him. Over it all, a singular message hammered in his brain.

The time was here.

The perpetrator had arrived. All Gabe had to do was cuff him and transport him to Interpol's New York office. Just like that. Simple, quick, and easy.

Except nothing about this case had been simple, quick, or easy. Why should he think the last phase would be?

He plopped on the edge of Mike's bed and tossed a sock in a pile of dirty laundry. Damn! What a mess. What an unbelievable muck he'd made of everything.

Even now, Gabe was avoiding the end. When he busted Hunter, it all fell apart: Victoria, Anastasia, Mike, and Jill. His hand raked through his hair to knead his neck. So what was he waiting for? Why hadn't he grabbed Hunter the minute he'd stepped through the door today?

Bust that guy, and your happy little family scene blows completely apart, you know. Yeah, he knew. He wasn't happy about it, but he knew.

Are you waiting for the Second Coming?

Time. He was waiting for the right time.

He wasn't upstairs postponing the inevitable while his lover served tea to the prey downstairs, he was biding his time. Besides, he didn't know what was in the package. He could wait a little longer.

"Hey, Gabe!" Mike called. "You going to sit there all day, or are you coming downstairs?"

He shot off the bed. "Right there, Mike."

"Hurry up. Uncle Bruce is here!"

"Ah, yes," Gabe drawled to himself. "Don't want to keep the good uncle waiting too long, do we?"

* * *

Seated at the patio table, Victoria wrangled with her brother. "This is ridiculous, Bruce. Mother's been anxiously waiting for your visit."

"Oh?" Bruce lifted an onyx brow in stark disbelief. "This year, last year, or a decade ago?"

Victoria gasped. "The least you can do is visit her. It's probably the last time you'll ever see her. With her heart, I doubt she makes it to Christmas."

He'd lost his mind, Victoria decided. Totally and completely. There had been marked changes since last year, none of them good, but she'd never known him to be callous.

"Mellow out, Vic," he said sharply before his attitude and features softened. "The mother of my heart died when this stupid disease took her mind. It tears me up to see her."

She couldn't argue with that. God knew Victoria didn't visit often, either. It was all so heartbreaking, so depressing, so hard.

"By the way, sis, I'm expecting a package before I head back." His demeanor was cool and nonchalant, but something in the set of his shoulders bespoke tension.

"Ah, yes, the mysterious package."

"It's here?" He threaded his hands together and grinned.

"Well, sort of . . ."

Bruce steepled his fingers and tapped them against his chin. "Sort of? What the devil is 'sort of'?"

"Well, it's hard to explain."

"Try." He smiled, but the word sounded as if it came through gritted teeth.

"It arrived last Tuesday—"

"Fabulous!" Bruce relaxed, and for the first time, seemed to really smile.

She hated to burst his bubble, but there wasn't any polite way to say it. "We can't find it. It disappeared."

"Wh-a-a-t?" Bruce asked in a low, cold voice. He grabbed Victoria's upper arm and jerked her forward. "Disappeared?"

"Bruce!" Victoria rolled her shoulder out of his grasp. "You're hurting me."

"The package," he rasped.

"Let her go," came a rough, low voice heavy-laden with warning. "She already told you we don't know where it is. It's gone."

Bruce turned cold eyes on Gabriel, who in turn smiled a feral grin Victoria hadn't known he possessed. Whenever the two men were within ten feet of each other, silent male signals she wasn't privy to passed between them. She shivered, almost as if someone had walked over her grave.

"If it turns up," her nanny said, "we'll let you know."

"Let me know?" Bruce shouted, and pushed away from the table to pace around the patio. "Are you all crazy?" He repeatedly raked agitated fingers through his well-coiffed hair. "No," he uttered, "of course not. I'm the one who's crazy. My God."

"Bruce?" Victoria stared, puzzled at the man who looked like her brother, but acted nothing like him. This man was in a frenzy, and she didn't know what to do to help.

Gabe watched the conversation. Hunter was a man on the edge. Just the way Gabe liked them, off balance.

"I need that package," Hunter said, his gaze flicking between his sister and Gabe.

The simple statement carried a wealth of innuendo Victoria didn't pick up on. Gabe heard what she couldn't, an edge, understated vehemence, and unhealthy fear. It was good for Gabe, but not the Devereauxs. Hunter's distraction proved the family was being used, possibly in danger. "I'll make a raid for it," he told Hunter, "turn the house upside down to find it. It's gotta be here."

Hunter's shoulders sagged in what might have been relief.

Gabe turned abruptly. "I've got to get supper started."

"Hey, man," Hunter called from behind him. "Thanks."

"My pleasure," Gabe returned without a hint of warmth. He wanted the package, too. A top priority. Seizing the envelope was the last thing he could do for the Devereauxs.

The house was finally quiet. All sane people were fast asleep by two A.M. From his bed, Gabe stared into the dark yard, unable to come up with anyplace he hadn't already searched. The missing package was his ace in the hole. It was obvious Hunter didn't have it, and Gabe was sure he wouldn't leave without it. Not after Hunter's reaction to its disappearance. The new turn of events gave Gabe more time, more breathing room.

He cursed the darkness and yanked the covers back. A prickle skidded across his shoulders, and he froze. The door shut with a click that echoed in his brain.

A soft, feminine chuckle floated through the darkness. "What's the matter, tough guy? Did I scare you?"

"Victoria," he breathed. "What are you doing here?"

She crossed the room and slid her arms around his waist. "I couldn't sleep."

He sighed. "Me, neither."

"I miss you," she said. Her nimble hands unerringly sought out all the places she'd learned the nights before. She was a quick study.

"I miss you, too, but this isn't the best idea." If she didn't leave soon, he wouldn't let her go. Every second pushed him toward the inevitable, and he wanted more, dammit, so much more. Could anyone blame him for basking in her light a little longer, for stealing a bit of her warmth? Everyone deserved a sliver of happiness. Even a cold bounty hunter.

"Hold me." In her husky voice, Gabe felt and heard the longing, the desire, the hope he would crush.

He held her close and dropped a chaste kiss on her head.

"Gabriel . . ." She stopped, took a deep breath, and began again. "I wanted to tell you—"

"Gabe! Gabe!" Anastasia's voice, sharp and piercing and terrified, broke his embrace. "No! No! Don't go!"

Victoria was out of his arms and halfway to the door. He shoved his legs into his jeans and tore down the hall behind her. A dim night-light cast tall shadows. Anastasia huddled in her mother's sheltering embrace, softly sobbing.

"What's the matter, short stuff?" he asked, settling on the bed next to them.

The child launched herself onto his lap and buried her face in his shoulder. Great, shuddering hiccups rocked her small body, and he met Victoria's gaze.

"She dreams you float away from her. The nightmares started Friday," Jill said, hovering uncertainly in the doorway. "Uncle Bruce said they were because she was away, and they'd stop when she got home."

Victoria trudged over to her oldest daughter and put

an arm around her shoulders. "Go back to bed, darling. There's nothing more you can do."

Gabe cuddled Anastasia close.

"Don't leave," she said.

"Then you'll have to come with me." The child still in his arms, he rose and settled into an old rocker. The rhythmic back-and-forth sway relaxed Anastasia, and her fingers eased off his arms. "Want to tell me about it? Sometimes bad dreams go away if you tell someone."

She shook her head, but the words tumbled from her lips. "We were in a yellow boat, and Mama, Uncle Bruce, Jillian, and Michael were in another. And there was bubbly water all around. Uncle Bruce fell out of the boat, and you went after him, but you didn't come back, and the water pulled me farther and farther away. You took Uncle Bruce on the shore, but you didn't come back to me," she said with a renewed burst of tears. "I was all alone 'cause you left me."

"Sh-h-h," he whispered. "It was a bad dream, sugar. I'm here," he soothed. "Nothing can hurt you now." Except me. Unnerved by the reality underlying her nightmare, he held her small body close and rocked in silence for several minutes. Her dream was grounded in reality. What could he say?

"Will my bad dream come true, Gabe?"

Dear God, he couldn't tell her the truth, and yet he couldn't lie to Anastasia. "I don't know, short stuff. I hope not."

"Me, too." She snuggled against him, burrowing her nose into his shoulder.

Gabe squeezed his eyes shut. His head rolled back on the high wood back of the chair. God help us, sweetheart. We're gonna need it.

* * *

"Let's get a move on, Vic," Bruce called from downstairs. "I don't want to waste any more time on this than necessary."

The impatience and aversion in his voice set Victoria's teeth on edge, but she tamped it down for her mother's sake.

Too bad Gabriel wasn't available to sing her a reassuring lullaby as he had to Anastasia last night. Her daughter had gotten the best part of the deal; she'd fallen asleep with him in the rocker. Victoria hadn't realized how empty a bed could be until then.

She didn't begrudge Anastasia the security and care Gabriel's arms offered. It was just that Victoria missed him. Terribly. Not just his body. This morning there wasn't the usual shower serenade, no wicked wink or throaty "Mornin'."

Then there was Bruce. Since he arrived, he'd been agitated, nervous, overwrought. Gabriel withdrew into a tense, glowering stranger in her brother's presence. Why?

"Five minutes, Vic! Or I'm not going!"

Attaching silver hoops on her ears, she shoved her good foot into a short pump. Thank goodness her ankle would be unwrapped in a few days. It was awkward and clumsy, and didn't help her mounting irritation. Heaven knew she'd need all the help she could get in dealing with the two men in her life. With that, she marched downstairs to her only brother.

Bruce's peevish behavior continued on the trip to the nursing home. He griped about having to drive, harped about her gypsylike earrings, and groaned about the futility of the visit. "I'm only doing it for you," he said with a snort.

Victoria glared at him. "As long as you do it, I don't care why."

Two silent blocks sped by before she broke the silence. "What's your problem? Something's eating at you."

He shrugged her off. "I'm fine."

He was anything but fine. Victoria hardly knew him. Obviously he wasn't willing to talk about it, and she wasn't in the mood for guessing games.

"Turn right at the next light. The parking lot is halfway down the block," she said.

Following her directions, Bruce sat in stony silence. His brooding continued as they walked side by side up the long concrete walk and through the glass doors. "This way," she said, and caught at his elbow to guide him along.

He eased out of her grip, and she sighed. "Look, Bruce, this isn't any picnic for me, either. Visiting Mother is the toughest thing I do. I'm not asking any more of you than I'm willing to give."

"No?" he asked with a silken sneer. "Deep down, you *like* it. You get off on all this family junk. I don't."

The statement was so absurd, she stared blankly at him. "You used to."

"No. You wanted to believe I did, so I let you." Halfway down the hall he stopped and smiled. "You're very good at that, you know. Believing what you want about a person. Doesn't have a lot to do with reality, but you see it the way you choose, Vic. Who am I to burst your rosy bubble?"

He spun on his heel and entered their mother's room. Victoria stood rooted in openmouthed astonishment.

"Mrs. Devereaux?"

Rousing herself, she glanced over her shoulder. The home's administrator, his few remaining gray hairs raked from one side of his balding head to the other, shifted from foot to foot. "Yes, Mr. Thacker," she said with a tentative smile.

"If you have a moment?" With a sober inclination of his head, he indicated his open office door.

"Of course." She followed him, her heel and brace emitting an odd click and thump into the quiet. Now what? Things couldn't possibly get worse.

"Mrs. Devereaux," the older man began. Seating himself behind a meticulously neat desk, he indicated a chair for her. His clasped hands rested, thin and quiet, on the clean blotter. "I know you're aware of your mother's precarious health. What you don't know is, two years ago, just after her fall and while she still had most of her mental faculties, she named you as having power of health care attorney."

He sounded tired, and Victoria didn't figure the news was good. Straightening her already straight spine, she prepared herself for the worst. "What does that mean?"

The administrator scrubbed his shiny upper lip with his index finger. "Nebraska doesn't recognize living wills. Having the power of health care attorney allows you to make all decisions concerning her health." Fixing her with a straight-on look, Thacker sighed. "If your mother codes—goes into cardiac arrest or any other life-threatening disaster—you must decide if you want her resuscitated, or allowed to expire with dignity."

Shock oozed through her veins. Her leaden heart thumped slow and heavy. Time stood still as the words settled in her mind. She was to decide her mother's death? To allow it or not? It was too much; the load was much too large. "My mother's put her life in my hands?"

"Only in an extreme circumstance."

"Why now?" Her voice trembled and her fingers

shook. Folding them in her lap, she tried unsuccessfully to still them.

"She's very frail," he said in a low, firm voice. "She could slip away at any time, and we have forms to be signed."

"Forms?" Victoria blinked at the man behind the desk, tried to focus on something tangible. "I can't sign any forms. It's too much. I—"

"Mrs. Devereaux, I know this is a shock. Don't give me a decision right now. Think about it, and let me know soon."

"What if she codes during the night? Shouldn't you be prepared?"

"We'll call you. I'm sorry, Mrs. Devereaux. I didn't mean to upset you." He stood dismissively, and Victoria groped blindly at the chair arms. She couldn't make such a decision alone. She had to discuss it with Bruce. Even as flaky as he'd become, they were family. It was their decision.

Wooden limbs carried her back to her mother's room. Bruce's voice, silky smooth and low, floated to meet her. As she neared the door, she frowned, the lines cutting deeper into her forehead. Her brother's elegantly cultured tones belied cruel, caustic words. "You're not doing either of us any good. We both know Vic and I would be better off if you were gone. I can't imagine what you're hanging on for."

What? She couldn't believe her ears. How could he say such a horrid thing? He had no right! No right at all to berate his own mother. He might have a high-stress job, a jet-setting life-style, and need R and R more than the rest of the working peasants, but it didn't give him the right to pass judgment.

The harsh retort on her lips died. She couldn't talk

to Bruce. She knew what his prejudicial answer would be. The choice fell back to her.

Victoria entered her mother's room. The elderly woman, more pale and frail since the last visit, raised vacant eyes. Her hands fidgeted with several swatches of brightly colored thread in her lap. She was always confused, and even though she didn't know the day or the year, Bruce had upset her.

Victoria's hands covered her mother's, and she gently untangled the needlepoint yarn. "Are you going to sew?" she quietly, soothingly asked the older woman.

A smile lit her mother's face. "Yes. I'm very good, you know."

"Yes, I know," she answered, tears filling her eyes. She ignored her brother's sarcastic snort.

Her mother patted her hand. Bony fingers covered with soft, paper-thin skin smoothed over Victoria's. The difference in their hands brought Victoria face-to-face with her mother's mortality and the life that lay in her hands. What directions should she give the staff?

One maverick tear trickled down her cheek. She wiped the moisture away.

"Enough, Vic. I'm outa here." With that, Bruce stormed out of the room.

Victoria settled her mother with the pretty threads, kissed her wrinkled forehead, and headed after her callous brother. She needed to discuss her upcoming decision with someone. It should be her brother, but her eavesdropped conversation told her what his answer would be. There was only one person she could trust, one person who would provide the empathy and understanding she needed.

She'd talk to Gabriel. Like the silent Sphinx, he was solid and unchanging. If ever there was a man she could trust, it was him.

TWELVE

"If your brother calls me Marvin once more, I won't be responsible for my actions." Gabriel's voice cut through the darkness of Victoria's bedroom.

She turned from the window to face him. "I apologize for his manners. He's never been such a jerk. I don't even know him anymore," she whispered. "But I'm glad you're here."

Long, strong fingers lifted a lock of her hair and smoothed it behind her ear. "I shouldn't be," he said.

She ignored the cold loneliness of his words, wrapped her arms around his waist, and laid her cheek on his chest. "Where else do you fit so perfectly?"

"Nowhere," he said. "That's the problem."

"Then why are you here?"

"I couldn't stay away," he murmured, and kissed her hair. "You've been preoccupied since you came home. What's up?"

She wanted, no, needed, to hear his words of comfort, if not love, some signal that he cared for her beyond the physical, something to fill her heart, validate her life. But if she couldn't share the burden with her brother, she couldn't dump it on Gabriel. "It doesn't matter."

He cupped her shoulders in his hands. "Yes, it does."

"Why?" she pressed.

A long silence passed, and she thought he hadn't heard. His fingers threaded in her hair, reeling her face toward him. "Because I care, dammit," he growled. "Too much."

His lips captured hers, and Victoria relaxed against him, allowing him full access to her mouth and body. His tongue sipped and swirled with a mastery that robbed her of coherent thought. His hands stole whatever remained behind. "Victoria!" he gasped. "God, I want you."

"Don't." Flattening a palm against his chest, she steadied herself. "I can't think when you kiss me."

He gathered a handful of her chintz robe and hauled her on tiptoe. "That makes two of us," he said, lowering his mouth to hers.

"Gabriel . . . please."

Releasing her, his roaming hands glided over her shoulders and chafed her upper arms, offering solace and sparking desire. "What is it, darlin'?"

"The nursing home informed me that my mother gave me power of health care attorney."

"What's that?" His breath tickled her ear.

"The power of life and death," she whispered. "If her health continues to deteriorate, they have to know whether or not to resuscitate if she . . . you know, codes."

Wrapping his arms around her shoulders, he drew her back against his chest. His warmth and strength encircled and enfolded her. Silent tears she'd held at bay through the day burst their dam, trickling down her face . . .

. . . and onto his wrist. Nothing had prepared Gabe for her tears. They scored his hard heart. He hadn't known how deeply he could feel someone else's pain. "Aw, Victoria. Don't. Don't cry."

"They're asking too much," she choked out. Damp tear trails shimmered on her cheeks. "I can't give the okay for my mother's death."

Her tears began anew, and Gabe held her close. For how long, he didn't know. Until she lapsed into dry shudders, his hands kneaded her back and communicated his impotent but genuine sympathy.

"What do I do?" she pleaded.

"I can't tell you that, babe." His thumbs swiped the tracks of her tears. "As much as I loved my wife and our baby, I wanted them to live, not exist. Watching that little bundle with tubes sticking out of her, lying in that incubator day in and day out, made me feel so helpless. I'd never want to put my family through that hell, but you've got to make the decision now. Once they're on life support, you sign on for the duration. Either way, it's hell."

"Why would she do this to me?"

He brushed a light kiss on her temple and stared into the black night with her. "Because she trusts you. And that trust is well placed."

"Would you allow me to make that decision for you?"

One heartbeat passed. Two. "In a minute, babe."

Her gaze meshed with his, silver-gray to stormy hazel, and she slipped her robe down her shoulders. "Make love to me, Gabriel. Please."

Flames licked his belly. She had that effect on him. Anytime, anywhere, she could turn him on in an instant. He should walk away, leave her alone, but there was no way. One last time, he needed to warm himself in her light, bathe himself in the salvation she offered his battered soul.

Taking her hand, he teasingly nipped her knuckles, fanning an ember of pleasure. He breathed a soft, moist kiss on her palm and closed her fingers around it one by one.

Her chemise pooled at her feet, and a tingling sensation feathered up from Victoria's toes to tickle the back of her throat. He lifted her in his arms and gently placed her on the bed.

Cool sheets cradled her backside; Gabriel's heat pressed against her breasts and belly. He moved his middle across hers, and the magic began anew. She framed his rugged face between her palms for a deep, lazy kiss, his raspy stubble abrading her sensitized fingertips. She sucked in a breath and moved sinuously against him, telegraphing her need for him.

"Keep your motor running, babe." He quickly shed his clothes and joined her. Smooth skin met hair-roughened skin. She sighed. He sighed.

"You feel good," she said. "So solid in this crazy, mixed-up world."

Gabriel laughed huskily. "Call me Gibralter, darlin'."

His hands drew slow, inching circles over her waist, up her sides. Her heart pounded erratically. Her stomach quivered in a rhythm directly proportionate to his thumbs skimming circles on her breasts.

"You are so beautiful," he murmured, and bit at her shoulder, "so wet and hot."

Victoria chuckled and tunneled her fingers through his silky brown hair. His tongue stroked at leisure, thoroughly exploring her mouth in a fever she more than returned. Hungrily she returned kiss for kiss, stroke for stroke, swirl for swirl. His mouth tasted her everywhere, his hands promising a beguiling, delicious madness that only he could deliver. "Now I know what melted Jell-O feels like," she said with a soft groan of pleasure. "You're driving me crazy."

"Lucky you," he rasped against her shoulder, "I've got a surefire cure." His fingers, intimately manipulating, slid down their bodies, seeking and finding the dewy dampness hidden within her. He stroked her downy softness and returned to her heated flesh again and again.

"Enough!" Victoria caught his hair in her hands and kissed him, molding her body to his.

"Wrong." His unsteady breath shuddered out. "It's not nearly enough, but it'll have to do."

Hot, ragged breaths twined, whispering through the night. Silently, worshipfully, they slipped into the slow, heated cadence of love, and Victoria tumbled headlong into a total fulfillment that surpassed anything that had gone before.

Lengthening fingers of light crept into Victoria's bedroom. The same morning sun woke Gabe and cut his time short. Today was the day to bust her brother, but he couldn't bring himself to leave just yet.

Pulling her sleepy warmth against him, he spooned his body around hers. He'd messed things up big time, and he'd miss the hell out of her, but there was nothing he could do.

The moment he stepped out of her bed, he'd set off an unstoppable chain reaction. She'd never want to see him again. His arms tightened around her as though he could stave off the inevitable, but of course, he couldn't. A few minutes, it would wait a few more minutes.

The digital clock on the nightstand ticked off the quickly moving time, silently counting down Gabe's demise. He steeled himself for what the day would bring. At least the kids would be at Bible school. He'd count that much a blessing, but he still had to maneuver Victoria out of the way before he cuffed Hunter. He'd save her that much.

Brushing her hair aside, he kissed the soft skin behind her ear. Ah, Victoria, I'm sorry. A sorry son of a bitch.

Setting his jaw at an angle Victoria had labeled arrogant, he slipped out of her bed and into his jeans. Slow, halting steps carried him to the door. His fingers curled into the frame, stopping him for one glance backward. Enough to drink in her loveliness to last him a long, long time.

"Now that you've made up your mind, you should sign the health care attorney stuff as soon as possible," Gabriel said. "I mean, no use putting it off, is there?"

Victoria turned to him with a wan smile. "Trying to get rid of me?"

"Of course not." His gaze shifted to where her brother sunned himself by the pool. "I just think today's as good as tomorrow for something this important."

His odd demeanor had confused her all morning. He was a touch withdrawn, cordially but coolly polite; no one would guess he was the ardent, passionate lover of last night, whispering hot words of mindless ardor, murmuring soft words of gentle desire. Since talking with him last night, she'd made up her mind. There was only one choice.

If the situation were reversed and it were Victoria in her mother's place, she would want the nursing home instructed, *no resuscitation*. Her choice for her mother was death with dignity, not machines. Rose's life, while not overly long, had been full and loving. It was the last thing Victoria could do for her.

But it seemed as if Gabriel was pushing, hovering, waiting, but for what? Then again, fatigue and stress had her jumping at shadows, seeing things where nothing existed. The strange behavior of the two men in her life and her mother's poor health were enough to put anyone over the edge.

"So?" Gabriel asked in a gentle nudge, but a nudge that irked Victoria just the same. "You could drive over this afternoon."

He'd taken her to get her cast off earlier that morning, and although she had the go-ahead to drive, the ankle was still tender. "Won't you come with me?"

Again his gaze drifted to her brother, and Gabriel shook his head. "I'd love to, but I've still got to find that stupid package for your brother."

"You can do that tomorrow." What had happened to bring about this shift? The men in her life were acting stranger and stranger each day, and she hadn't a clue as to why.

"No, I can't." His gaze drilled into hers. The words held finality, and chilled Victoria to her bones. "I can't."

"I see," she said, but didn't see anything except Gabriel's increasing isolation from her. "I might as well go now as later."

Gabe breathed a sigh of relief. For a minute there, he thought she'd dig in her stubborn heels and stick around. He glanced at his watch. Things were proceeding right on schedule, he thought, and scaled the stairs two at a time.

Zipping his well-packed duffel bag, he glanced around his room one last time. A quickly scribbled note—although it could never fully explain or apologize—and his uncashed paychecks sat on his pillow, a ruffly thing that reminded him too much of Victoria. His hand shook, and he immediately fisted the fingers. Jaw clenched, he headed downstairs. No use postponing the inevitable.

Hunter had moved from pool to family room, lounging on a recliner, lazily flicking the cable remote control. He glanced at Gabe's stoic presence. A ripple of unease passed through Hunter's eyes before he quickly covered it. "Well, well, Marvin. Leaving so soon?"

Gabe dropped the bag and the pretense. "Yes," he said, and reached out to grab Hunter's shirt and haul him bodily out of the chair. "*We* sure are."

"Let go, you neanderthal. I'll have you arrested so fast, your head will swim."

The man could bluster, Gabe thought. A real handy skill in the weasel's line of work. Before Hunter could blink, Gabe had him spread-eagle facing the chair. Gabe reached for the handcuffs, and took a sharp elbow in his still tender ribs, forcing him to release his prey. "You wanna play rough, sucker?" Gabe snarled. "You got it."

The two men circled each other in the family room. Gabe figured Hunter had cunning and wiles but no brawn or street smarts.

He figured right.

Two upper cuts to Hunter's glass jaw, a few grunts and groans, and the jerk was helpless. Pressing a knee into Hunter's back, Gabe slapped on the cuffs, tightening them as much as he could. "Let's go, jerk," he said, and hauled Hunter up by his belt.

"This is false arrest," Hunter spat. A tiny trickle of blood spotted the corner of his big mouth. "Where's your warrant? Where's my rights?"

"You're a frigging fugitive from justice," Gabe growled. "And I'm the bounty hunter. I don't need a warrant, and you got no rights with me, my man. None at all." He shoved the hand–shackled man in front of him. "Now, move it."

The front door swung open. A breathless Victoria barreled into the room and stopped in her tracks.

No! God, no! She's supposed to be gone. It's not supposed to be this way. It didn't matter what had happened or why she was here. Gabe'd pushed his luck once too often and much too far.

"Bruce, what happened to your face?" Her startled gaze spiraled to Gabe. "What's going on, Gabriel?"

"Boy, you did it this time, little sister." Hunter sneered. "The jerk you hired as a nanny is arresting me."

Her eyes widened, her chin jutting at a hard angle. "Don't be ridiculous."

Her brother spun around to show her his cuffed hands. "Is this ridiculous enough for you?"

"Gabriel?" She pressed a hand to her chest as though she struggled for air. "What's he talking about?"

"Victoria . . . I—"

"I trusted you, Vic," her brother interjected. "I thought I was safe in your home." He tossed a disgusted look at Gabe, who stood silent, "I was wrong."

"Safe from what?" she shrieked. "What's going on!"

"Your nanny isn't a nanny, sis. He's a bounty hunter. He only came to lay a trap for me."

The condemnation in Victoria's eyes held Gabe captive. "Is that true?" she asked softly, far too softly.

"Yes. I'm sorry," he muttered. It was a lame excuse, but it was all he had.

"Sorry?" she shouted. "Then you are arresting Bruce? For what?"

"He's a fugitive from international justice," Gabe blazed back. "I'm licensed to bring in the bad guys. It's my job."

"Oh really?" Cynicism, so unlike her, boiled beneath the surface of her words and cut Gabe to the heart. "Are deceit, lies, and seduction part of your job, too?"

He took a step toward her, one palm outstretched. "Victoria, you know that's not true."

She turned to look at him—as if she were just now seeing clearly. Tears spangled her silvered eyes. "Do I?" She spun around, hugging her arms to her. "What were you going to do, haul my brother off to jail and rush back before I found out?"

Grinding his teeth in total frustration, Gabe said nothing.

"Well?" she demanded.

He pulled her brother toward the door. "I have to take him to Interpol in New York."

She blocked the way. "Why? What did he do?"

"Industrial espionage, among other things, if you must know—"

"I must," she grated. "What else?"

"He's a fancy thief who sells his booty to the highest bidder!" Gabe hollered over the blood pounding in his ears.

"I see," she said, totally calm and supposedly collected.

Gabe knew better. He knew her too well to let her go like this. But he wouldn't have to let her go; she'd boot him out. He'd known that all along, prepared himself for it. No amount of imagining had prepared him for the pain in her eyes, in her words, in his heart.

"And were you coming back, Gabriel?" Her words demanded, her eyes implored.

"No." His answer hung in the air.

"You sure can pick 'em, baby sis."

Victoria and Gabe ignored the jibe. Each focused totally on the other. "Don't do this, Gabriel," she pleaded.

Had she asked anything else, anything at all, he would've moved heaven and earth to do it. But this— "I can't. He broke the law, and he's got to answer for it."

"It isn't possible—"

"It is!" Gabe had played the scene before. Always the undying belief of the family in the poor sucker's behalf, and always misplaced.

"I'll do anything," she said, "anything you want, anything you ask. Just name it. Just don't take my brother. He's all I've got. Gabriel, you know that."

"I can't. He's a fugitive, a criminal, for God's sake." He pushed Hunter in front of him again, hoping to make it to the door before she broke down completely. If that happened, Gabe would be torn in half. Unable to complete the bust, unable to leave Victoria. "We've got a plane to catch."

"No!" Flinging her hands horizontally, she blocked their progress. "Please, Gabriel," she said quietly, visibly struggling for calm and composure. "I'm begging you."

Her quicksilver gaze full of heartache and confusion tugged at Gabe's heart. For her own good, and his, he had to end it and leave. Now. "Good-bye," he said quietly.

Victoria stood aside, not uttering another word. Her chin was tilted at a royal angle, only one tremble belying her outward composure. Nothing had ever cut

Gabe so deeply. He towed Hunter onto the porch. The door calmly clicked shut behind him. He'd done it, but he wasn't congratulating himself. He'd hurt her and damned himself.

On the short trip to Eppley Airport, Gabe held himself together with the thinnest, most brittle thread.

"Nice going, Marvin. You've got a real way with women." Lowering his voice to a confidential level, he sneered. "Vic's gonna hate you forever."

A thousand emotions swirled and crashed inside Gabe, a tidal wave of emptiness. Not that he didn't deserve it, but it still hurt like hell. "I didn't expect anything less," he growled, glaring at Hunter with lethal intensity. "And don't call me Marvin again. On a good day, I'd make your life miserable, but today . . . don't push me."

Good-bye. Gabriel's parting words keened through Victoria's mind. He'd left her, taken her brother away. What would she tell the children? How would she explain this?

On the heels of disillusionment came the hurt. Dear God, it hurt. Her whole world had gone wild, and then dead. How could he do this to her when she'd loved him so much? Since when was love ever enough?

She walked through the empty house in a stupor of anguish. His room drew her, like a bee to a rose, like a lover to the beloved. Resting her head on the doorframe, she surveyed the tidy, empty room and spied a white envelope bearing her name in bold, spartan strokes. Four weekly paychecks—uncashed—wrapped in a white sheet of paper fell out. His last words were scrawled in front of her. *"I'm sorry."* Tears brimmed in her eyes. She was tired, so tired and more alone than she'd ever been. She allowed them to fall. A flood of sad tears with millions more to follow.

"Uncle Bruce did somethin' bad?" Michael asked at supper.

"Pretty bad, I guess," Victoria answered. "I don't have any details."

"Gabe is a bounty hunter?" Jillian asked in a totally scandalized teenage way. "Aren't they from the old West?"

"Obviously not," she replied.

"When's Gabe coming back, Mama?" Anastasia's question was the hardest. She'd loved Gabe openly and honestly. She didn't deserve his betrayal. None of them did.

"He's not, sweetheart. He's—"

"Yes he is!" the child shouted, and burst into tears. "He is, he is, he is!"

Victoria got through the evening without breaking down. How, she'd never know. Mental numbness, an insulating cocoon of shock, enveloped her. With a clear eye, she finally saw the jumbled pieces of the past few days fall together.

Everything fit now—Gabriel's withdrawal, Bruce's preoccupation, the general tension she felt but couldn't pin down—all clicked in a hideous picture of deceit and lies.

Staring out her bedroom window into the night's gloom, she realized she was searching for the familiar orange glow of his cigarette. Try as she might, she couldn't summon up the appropriate outrage for the occasion. Bruce had changed, and she'd noted the difference immediately. That he'd broken the law, or done whatever required a bounty hunter to trail him, didn't surprise her, not as much as it should.

She could forgive Gabriel the masquerade, the lies, her brother, almost anything. But he'd left her, just like before. The only difference was, this time she wasn't pregnant. Was she?

Memories of their nights together flashed through her mind. She wasn't an irresponsible teenager, she was a woman who'd been celibate for over six years, who hadn't given a thought to procreation. Her hand splayed protectively across her womb. Maybe this time wasn't different after all.

On the East Coast, Gabe stepped onto the balcony of his fancy New York City hotel room. A fifth of whiskey dangled from his fingers. He lifted the bottle to his lips and filled his mouth with the liquor. It blistered its way down his throat, hitting his empty stomach like a fireball. His lips pulled back in a grimace while a shudder racked his body.

Good bust. Good flight. Good whiskey.

The day had been hell.

He lit a cigarette. That luxury had been taken away from him a month ago, and now it was time to get back on track. If only he could erase the scent, the texture, the feel of Victoria Devereaux, from his memory.

He glared down at his cigarette. It gave him something to do with his hands, but it tasted like crap. Unbuttoning his shirt, he cursed the humidity, the big city, and the pollution for his sleeplessness and short temper.

He ground thumb and forefinger against closed lids. His eyes burned, and his gut was a sea of acid. A steady hammer beat an anvil inside his head. Probably the flu.

Or something worse.

Gabe downed another healthy swallow, braced himself for the coming blitz, and calmly faced the truth. He'd fallen in love with Victoria Devereaux. Hell, he'd fallen for the whole damn family. One by one, like little dominoes, they'd battered down his well-constructed barriers.

The amber bottle journeyed to his mouth again, and he prayed for a drunken stupor. Anything to rid his mind of the Devereauxs and relieve his aching heart.

He'd wanted a home, more than anything, but he was afraid of screwing it up again. The first time Providence had smiled on him, he hadn't been able to protect his wife or his daughter. Death was easy; survival was hell.

This time one thing would be different. By nailing Hunter, Gabe had prevented him from involving Victoria and her crew in anything further. At least they were safe. Never mind that he was drowning in misery.

THIRTEEN

A phone was ringing. Somewhere nearby. Too damn loud. If Gabe let it alone, the irritating noise would stop. But what about the pounding in his head?

Early afternoon light pierced the draperies and penetrated his eyelids. Confused, he cracked open one eye and glanced around the bed. Empty. Victoria? Damn! Victoria.

He flopped onto his stomach and held his throbbing temples. Would his first thoughts in the mornings always be of Victoria?

The river of booze he'd downed last night hadn't dulled the pain of walking out on her, hadn't burned away the haunting betrayal in her eyes, hadn't cauterized the gaping wound in his own heart.

He was richer, freer, and lonely as hell. When would he learn? Surviving didn't make you special or worthy, it made you feel like hell.

The irritating *b-r-n-n-g, b-r-n-n-g, b-r-n-n-g* continued. "Shut up," he growled at the offensive telephone, then flipped to his back and groaned. "Let me die in peace."

Three more rings passed before Gabe knocked the phone to the floor with a specific curse about its ancestry. "Sanders! Sanders? You ugly SOB, answer!"

Gabe glared at the floor. Only Rick knew he was here. Reluctantly he scooped up the receiver. "Yeah?"

"Really tied one on, huh?" Rick said. "Must've been a great collar."

"Yeah," Gabe agreed dryly, "helluva collar. You calling from across the ocean just to harass me?" He rubbed his stubbled chin and settled into the pillows.

"Sorry I couldn't be there."

"I'm a big boy, Parrish. I don't need you to baby-sit."

"So everything went down smooth as Irish whiskey?"

A moment's hesitation betrayed Gabe. "Yeah," he agreed quickly. "Real smooth." So smooth, I tripped myself up.

"Good. Then you found those canisters of Hunter's."

Tightness twisted in Gabe's belly, putting him on his guard. "What canisters?"

"Film containers. The jerk spread himself too thin. Double-crossed one corporation, counterspied for a couple of Middle East big shots." Rick paused. "Dumb bastard."

"And the film?"

"Direct evidence to nail the case shut tighter than a fresh coffin."

"And?"

"Bring a peck of trouble if it falls into the wrong hands."

Gabe rubbed at the jackhammer in his head. "The stuff disappeared a week ago. I tore the damn place apart trying to find it, but no dice."

"Better let the lady know to keep her eyes peeled and give us a jingle if she finds it."

"Why?" Gabe asked, instinctively knowing he wouldn't like the answer.

"Because the guys Hunter deals with won't be nice about retrieving it. Mrs. Devereaux should probably install extra security just in case."

"The Devereauxs are in danger?"

"Only if the wrong folks know it's there."

Gabe swore explicitly, fluently. Victoria and the kids might be in danger. He had to go back.

A thousand miles away, Victoria leafed through the ledgers, files, and updated product information. Even getting ready to rejoin the work force didn't enthuse her. She had accomplished one thing, living through twenty-four hours without Gabriel Sanders.

Each moment without him hurt, each thought about him hurt. Every beat of her heart hurt. Unbearably. Miserably. The future didn't look much better. She tried to summon self-righteous anger, but didn't have the energy.

All she could muster was an engulfing sadness that overwhelmed her. Anger and guilt would wait. She had her hands full struggling under a load of emptiness. Empty like his room, her bed, and her soul. Endlessly empty. Only Gabriel could fill her again. And he wasn't coming back.

You sure can pick 'em, Vic.

Yeah, she sure could.

Gabe caught the first flight back. He looked and felt like hell, and scowled at the flight attendants until they left him blessedly alone. How much worse could things get? Even O'Hare Airport's insanity was simpler than the task ahead of him. He'd be *persona non grata* at the Devereaux's. His nightmare come true. So quit bitching and take your medicine.

The plane landed in Omaha, and Gabe wound his way through the building like a man with a mission.

Springing into his car, he roared off to Victoria's. What he'd say, he didn't know; how he'd convince her to let him stay, he didn't know; how he'd keep from pulling her into his arms, he didn't know. He'd done it once, he'd do it again.

The miles sped by, and Gabe's heart hammered erratically. Adrenaline, he wondered, or plain old love? Within ten minutes, he was there. *Home.* The word popped into his head unbidden, like the contentment surging through his veins.

Hurt my children . . . I'll never forgive you. . . . She's gonna hate you . . .

Gabe plodded up the front steps. Hate or no hate, he couldn't leave them unprotected, not while he drew breath. She could make book on it.

Westminster chimes pealed through the quiet house. Victoria's heart lurched; fear skittered along her spine. What now? she wondered, recalling the lost package, the lying nanny, the odd noises last night.

Don't be stupid, Victoria. It's nothing. She was jumping at shadows again, and it was getting ridiculous. She'd handle this without him, without Gabriel, the bounty hunter who'd carted her brother off. The man she loved.

The caller dispensed with the polite formality of the bell and resorted to a barbaric pounding on her door. "I'm coming, I'm coming," she hollered.

Her hand hovered over the knob. Apprehension scraped along her nerves. Shoving it aside, she yanked the door open. "Yes, what is it?"

"Victoria."

Her startled gaze flew to the well-beloved face, and for a moment, drank in unsmiling lips, tired eyes, and spiritless voice. Gabriel was back. Hope flared, then died.

She needed to do something. Quick. Before she did something stupid like tumble into his arms and welcome him home. Dormant anger flared to life, sweeping through her at a blistering pace. She wrapped it protectively around her battered heart. "Forget something, or just returning to the scene of the crime?"

His jaw clamped shut at a bone-grinding angle. "We need to talk."

"There's nothing more to say." She moved to slam the door in his face. A strong arm braced against the middle, his sneakered foot wedged against the bottom, and she couldn't budge it. "Really, Gabriel!"

"You need to hear the whole story."

Emptiness flashed through her, a yearning for what might have been. She steeled herself against such softness. "Save the strong-arm tactics for your victims. Go away before I call the police and have *you* arrested."

"I'll just show them my ID and they'll let me go. Dammit, stop pushing on the door! We need to talk."

"Go—"

A car door slammed behind him. Glaring at each other, neither noticed. Anastasia bounded across the lawn and up the stairs. "Gabe! Gabe! You're back. You're home."

Anastasia wrapped her arms around his knees in a familiar hug of affection. Victoria swallowed hard, and blinked sudden moisture away. Don't make this harder. "Why are you home from Bible school so soon?"

"I told 'em I thought I hadda throw up."

Before Victoria could release the door, Gabriel

swung her daughter into his arms. They looked as if they'd plotted the scene for a week. Or he loved her.

Anastasia squeezed his neck and planted a moist, smacky kiss on his cheek. "I missed you. Where did you go?"

"Uh, darling." Victoria hoped to stem her daughter's growing bubble of happiness. "Gabriel isn't staying long—"

"Yes, I am," he said, beaming at Anastasia.

"And you're not feeling well," Victoria continued as though she hadn't heard him, "so let's get you upstairs."

"I'm not sick," the child protested. "I was bored."

"Uh-huh," Victoria said, and pried her away from Gabriel.

"Gabe always takes care of me. I want Gabe!"

"Anastasia!" Victoria cringed. "I'm your mother."

"I know," the child said, tears filling her tender eyes. "But I love Gabe, too."

Defeated, Victoria stepped back and motioned Gabe in. He carried the child upstairs to settle her in bed.

Downstairs, Victoria paced. Why was he here? Hadn't he done enough? Did he need to completely destroy her?

"She's down for a nap at least," he said quietly, startling Victoria anyway. "I doubt it's anything other than terminal boredom."

"Thank you so much," Victoria said coldly. "Where did you say you got your medical training?"

"The police academy. A long time ago." Gabriel sprawled in an easy chair much the same as he had several days ago. As if he owned the place.

"You're a cop?" Victoria said with disbelief. Caught between wanting to know everything about him and knowing it would only make things harder. Again.

"Used to be."

She didn't want to care anymore, but she did. He had to go—now. "I'll see you out."

"Sit down, Victoria." It was a quiet, softly spoken order, but an order just the same.

She crossed her arms. "I don't take directions from you."

"Really," he said with an arrogant slant to his brows. "You took them real well the other night."

Heat flooded her cheeks, and she damned his ungentlemanly reminder of their lovemaking. He'd told her he wasn't a nice guy. She was beginning to believe him.

"What do you want?" she asked simply.

You, in a thousand different ways. The phrase popped to mind before he could douse it. Before a million unbidden fantasies joined it, Gabe reined his thoughts back. "There's a loose end to this situation."

"And you're here to tie it up," she offered, eyeing him with calculating speculation. "Get whatever you need," she finally said with a sigh. "Then get out."

Her attitude was his penance. Every word she threw his way, every icy glare, every moment in her company, would be pure hell. It was no less than he deserved, so he'd accept it, finish the job, and do as she asked. Get out. "It's not that easy, Victoria. I need that package."

"I don't know where it is. You already know that."

Exasperated to the fraying point, he slapped his hands on his thighs. "Well, *somebody* knows where it is. It can't disappear into thin air."

"Exactly what my brother thought."

He raked his fingers through his hair. "I won't apologize for busting your brother."

"I wouldn't expect you to." She stiffened. Her crossed arms seemed to be all that held her together.

Gabe longed to kiss away the pain, but the woman didn't want him.

Victoria had never wanted him more. Not only sexually, but emotionally. She'd tasted the heights of passion with him and was addicted to the narcotic of his presence. But once he got the package, he'd leave again.

"Has there been anything unusual going on around here?" he asked. "Funny phone calls, attempted breaking and entering, strange people at the door?"

"Just you," she said with a too bright grin. She'd be darned if she'd run to him with fears and suppositions. She'd call the police if things really got bad.

"Very funny," he said.

They stared across the room at each other, former lovers, current opponents. The grandfather clock tick, tick, ticked, finally chiming out the quarter hour. Victoria detected tension in him, read the almost unreadable glint in his eyes. Her heart drummed a heavy beat. He looked hard, cynical, reckless. And sexier than sin.

Gabe noted the unnatural stiffness in her stance and wondered how much more strain she could take before she crumpled. "This isn't getting us anywhere," he said. "I need that package."

"Why?" Anger bubbled over again, and she shot him a searing look. "And this time, try the whole truth."

Gabe studied her a long moment. She deserved nothing less than the best. That wasn't him. "Sit." She stood her ground. "Sit, or I won't explain anything."

Plunking down on the sofa, she glared in open mutiny and let him know she was only there under duress. "Talk."

"I said I used to be a cop," he began. She nodded, encouraging him on. "That was my job when Diane and the baby died. I went heavy into self-pity and booze, got myself suspended from the force, and kept right on boozing until a friend of mine helped me wake up and drink the coffee." He glanced at her and received another encouraging nod, as if she suspected spilling his guts didn't come easily.

"The friend's name was Rick Parrish, a fellow officer. He helped me get my stuff together, and between us and our contacts, I became a bail bondsman.

"That's what I am. A month ago, Rick called. He's with Interpol—international police. Your brother jumped bail and the country. Under those circumstances, I become a bounty hunter. I can cross state lines, do whatever's necessary to bring the fugitive—your brother—in." He hesitated. "I owed Parrish a personal favor, so I took the case."

"How did you know I needed a nanny?" she asked quietly.

Gabe raked his fingers through his hair again. "Good informants. Mine and Interpol's."

"How did you happen to be the only candidate left?"

He ducked his head and cursed. "I called in some debts and got the others hired away."

Victoria gasped.

"I would've done anything to get your brother."

She paused, as though considering his statement. "Was seduction part of the case?"

"I didn't accomplish it all by myself, now did I?" His anger spit to life and quickly died. "Look, Victoria—"

"Why do you need the package?" she interrupted.

"Because it puts you and the kids in danger."

Victoria sprang to her feet and strode to the fireplace. "How long will it take to find it?"

"I don't know. I want to wrap this up quickly."

A weak smile plucked at her lips. "I'll bet you do. Fine. Stay here as a guest until we find it."

Gabe was so relieved, it didn't occur to him until later that she hadn't questioned how he knew they were in danger.

"I've got supper on the way," he told her six hours later. "Go wash up," he called to the kids.

"I'm perfectly capable of getting a meal," Victoria said.

"Oh, yeah?" he returned. "Then set the table. Casual."

"You're *not* the nanny anymore," she said, pulling down glasses and plates despite her irritation. "I resent you marching in here as though nothing has happened."

"I'm well aware of everything that happened."

Her stomach twisted with the memories of his love-making. But other things had been happening over the past two days, things Gabriel had no knowledge about, strange things. There would be snow at the equator before she'd confide in him, but he was here, and he'd mentioned danger. He was right.

Supper was quiet and subdued. Anastasia gazed at Gabriel with undiluted adoration. Jillian and Michael said little and picked at their food. Gabriel remained withdrawn and tight-lipped.

"Why did you take my uncle away?" Michael blurted into the heavy silence.

Gabriel laid his fork down and propped his fist under his chin. "He broke some laws, Mike, and he ran away from the police. They asked me to bring him back."

"You didn't have to," Jillian burst out. "You could've said no."

Before Victoria could intervene, Gabriel glanced at her, an unfathomable sadness in his eyes. "No, Jill. I couldn't. Look, you guys, your uncle isn't a bad man. Sometimes money makes people do crazy things, and then they get into bad situations. I'm sure he loves you all very much," he said with a thick, husky voice. "He didn't mean to hurt you."

Another sticky silence hung over the table. Victoria couldn't finish her meal. Food wouldn't pass through the lump in her throat. Gabriel had passed up the perfect opportunity to blacken her brother, call him names and reel off his offenses against society. Instead, he justified Bruce in a gentle way, and saved her children's pride. He felt the anguish of her children. It was written all over his face.

And he was hiding something else.

The telephone rang, halting the Devereauxs midaction. Gabe couldn't help but notice the faltering moment. Something was definitely wrong with the picture. By the second ring, he pushed out of his chair.

"I'll get it," Victoria said a moment too late.

"Forget it." Something was going on. Something Victoria hadn't let him in on. Something she'd lied to him about. Okay, not technically lied, but omitted. No wonder she hadn't fought harder against him coming back. He jerked the phone off the hook. "Yeah?"

"Hunter?" a woody voice on the other end wheezed.

"Who the hell wants to know?" Gabe growled.

"It doesn't matter. I want my stuff, and I want it now."

"Sorry," Gabe barked. "Dunno what you're talking about."

"My sources say otherwise."

"Yeah?" Gabe returned. "Your sources don't know squat." He slammed the receiver down and turned to the Devereauxs. "Okay, out with it. How long has this garbage been going on?"

Jill opened her mouth to speak, but her mother cut her off. "Since the evening you took Bruce away."

Her words held no rancor, no accusation, and Gabe breathed a sigh of relief. If he didn't have to fight her, things would be a lot easier. "Anything else?"

"Funny noises at night," Anastasia piped.

Gabe's brows lifted. "What funny noises?"

"We didn't think they were anything," Victoria offered. "But then . . ."

"What?"

"Come with me." She stood and led the way to the patio and pushed the French doors together.

A faint jimmy mark marred the finish, and he frowned. "What else?"

"Isn't that enough?" she asked.

Gabe nodded. He could kill Hunter for involving them in a volatile situation. "I'm sorry," he said. "I didn't know this would be dangerous to you or the kids. I'll do my damnedest to clean the whole mess up."

He extended his large hand to her. "Truce?"

Victoria hesitated. He made it all sound so neat and tidy, but there was more to be reckoned with. Knowing she could never turn her back on him or anything he asked, she placed her hand in his and was immediately engulfed in his familiar warmth. His skin scraped along hers. He cupped her palm, fondled her fingers.

"Victoria . . ."

She heard the incredible longing, the apology he couldn't voice, the reality of the present situation. "Truce," she said, and eased her hand from his. "Besides, there was no real damage done."

Not unless you include my heart, Gabe thought, and watched her slip back into the house.

By two A.M., Victoria knew it would be another sleepless night. Snuggled on the bay window's cushioned seat, she stared outside with sightless eyes. She'd been overconfident, too smugly assured that she could go on without him.

She'd fallen into the typical female trap, assuming a man loved you if he made love to you. Correction, if he had sex with you. No, a deep, inner part of her disagreed. Gabriel made love, and you know it.

Drawing her feet up under her, she sighed. Yes, she knew it. If he hadn't voiced undying love, so be it. He'd brought it to her in small ways during the days and large ways at night. She didn't begrudge a moment with him, only the fact that she had to give him up. Again.

Across the hall, sleep eluded Gabe as well. How he ever let her ascend the stairs and go to her own room, he'd never know. She was allowing him to stay here for one purpose, to wrap the whole situation up, and then she wanted him out.

He sighed and paced the moonlight-dappled room. On his return to the window, Gabe swore he saw a shadow slip between the large maple and linden trees in the backyard. He wasn't certain. Then he heard it. A creak, a rustle, definitely a noise that shouldn't be there in the wee morning hours.

Quickly, stealthily, he opened his duffel bag and slipped out a state-of-the-art automatic nine-millimeter Smith & Wesson. A soft snick confirmed a full clip of hollow-points. Edging down the hall, he eased the cartridge home, sparing a look toward Victoria's quiet room.

That's a good girl. Stay asleep.

Easing down the stairs, Gabe stopped and cocked his ear, waiting for the elusive sound again. *Brus-s-h. Cli-ck.*

He paused. The noise centered . . . in the kitchen? His surveying gaze searched the family room; finding it clear, he skittered to the wall. *Brus-s-h. Cli-ck.*

Inching toward the kitchen threshold, he drew in two steady breaths and blew them out slowly. Adrenaline bubbled in his veins, his heart pounding with a TNT charge. He'd blow away anyone who threatened this family. *Brus-s-h. Cli-ck.*

That someone was here. Gabe turned the corner and aimed the weapon at the ethereal figure in the center of the room. "Hold it right there," he snarled.

Hand pressed to her chest, a startled Victoria spun around and stared down at the gun barrel. A silver knife piled high with mayonnaise clattered to the floor. A half-made sandwich lay on the counter. She squeaked in surprise, then moaned. "I—oh . . ."

Gabe knew the look, the sound. He grabbed her just as she slithered away in a dead faint. "Jesus, Mary, and Joseph. Helluva night for a midnight snack."

He carried her into the den, placed her on the sofa, and went for a cool washcloth. Muttering a fluent string of curses, he gently bathed her pale face. "Come on, Vicki, darlin'," he prompted. "Wake up."

Consciousness hit Victoria with a blinding headache. "Don't call me Vicki," she snapped at the intruding voice. Memories flooded back. Not being able to sleep. The kitchen. Pouring a tumbler of chocolate milk. Making a simple cheese sandwich, and looking down the barrel of a gun. Someone had a gun in her house!

Her carefully constructed composure, held together by sheer will over the past few days, shattered, exploded in uncontained fury. Fingers curled into fists, she directed her ire at the closest object.

"Damn you!" she screamed, and hammered Gabriel's hard chest. He accepted it, making no move to stop her. Blow after blow rained down. "Damn you, damn you!" she spat. "You lied to me; you lied to my children; you lied to get into my house. I hate you. Do you hear me? I hate you!"

She loved him. Unbearably. But she couldn't stop, couldn't regain control of her flailing fists, or the words that tumbled in their wake. "You brought a big, ugly gun into my home. You have no right, do you hear? No right! You came here . . . and made us love you. I didn't want to, but I do, damn you, I do . . ."

The admission stunned him; long hours in his own personal hell galvanized him into action. He anchored her hands between one of his. Emotion radiated between them. Gabe fought for control, but emotions he'd wrestled into silence surfaced. "You think I wanted this?" he asked hoarsely. "I didn't. I didn't want to love you, either, but it happened. I didn't put this family in danger." He jerked her wrists and pulled her close. "I didn't steal and sell secrets. I didn't involve you in my slimy schemes."

Shut up, he told himself, shut up! But the wall had been breached, and he couldn't hold back. "That big, ugly gun is the only thing protecting you and the kids. The threat isn't from my weapon, babe. It's from those jerks your brother double-crossed. He brought this on, not me."

Gabe's voice rose with each declaration until he was shouting. He grabbed her delicate shoulders and shook her. "Don't you get it yet?"

She struggled against his tight hold. "Yes, damn you. Yes!"

A tiny, ineffectual tug on his bicep caught Gabe by surprise. Anastasia, tears running down her cheeks, was trying to pry his hands off her mother. "Stop, Gabe," she said, gulping big, sobbing breaths. "Leave my mama alone."

Gabe stared down at his hands, Victoria's pale face, Anastasia's tearful one. He released Victoria and pushed off the sofa to pace in front of the fireplace. "I—I'm sorry," he said, instantly appalled at his outburst. "I know sorry's not much, but—"

Molly's "who-o-ff" broke the tension, and riveted Gabe's attention to the backyard. He stole to the French doors, peeling back a sliver of curtain. A lone figure hesitated behind the diving board. A large figure. Possibly a man. Molly snarled and barked, pacing inside her pen.

Victoria followed Gabe's line of vision. "What is it?"

"You and Anastasia stay here. I'll be right back." Drawing his weapon again, Gabe skulked onto the patio. God help the poor bastard dumb enough to be out there.

Molly paced in her pen, whined, and barked. Gabe could barely make out anything distinct, but the dog focused on a point to his left and growled low in her throat. Good dog.

Hunching down low, he sprinted around the building. Directly ahead was the quarry. A man, and apparently not very bright. He stood tall, as though scouting the front of the house. Gabe swung an arm around the man's throat, his thumb pushing into the Adam's apple. He nudged the nine-millimeter into the creep's ear. "One sound, and you're yesterday's garbage."

"Wha—"

Gabe spun the man against the side of the garage

and kicked his legs apart. A quick pat-down showed a concealed switchblade. "A real sweetheart," Gabe said, and notched the cuffs as tight as they would go.

"Who the hell are you?" the intruder asked.

"Who were you expect—" The world burst into a kaleidoscope of brightly colored spots and stars before Gabe slid into unconsciousness.

"Jeez, Charlie," the handcuffed man breathed. "S'about time. I thought I was done for. Get me outta here."

Charlie rifled through Gabe's jeans pockets. "Where the devil did he put the key?"

"What was he doing with handcuffs in the first place?"

"Listen," Charlie said. "You hear something?"

"A baby bawling maybe?" the other man scoffed. "We cased this place two days ago. There's just a woman and a bunch'a kids. Get a move on, you idiot."

"I'm telling you, the key isn't here!"

Victoria had no intention of being rescued, certainly not by an underhanded bounty hunter—no matter how much she loved him. This was her home, her children, and her brother's mess.

That's why she'd stopped in the garage and grabbed the closest, biggest, heaviest piece of equipment she could reach. Michael's baseball bat. She'd never hit another human being before tonight. First Gabriel, and now whoever was invading the privacy of her home.

The voices hadn't been soft, which made them easy to follow. Her fingers tightened around the solid piece of wood, and she edged around the back of the house as she'd seen Gabriel do when he'd left them in the family room. Turning the corner, she stifled a gasp. One quick glance showed three men; one handcuffed, one squatting, one facedown on the ground. Gabriel. Oh my God. Gabriel!

Fury spurted through her. It was one thing for her to hit him, something entirely else for someone else to hit him. And so hard! The other men seemed oblivious to her, so she stalked up behind the uncuffed one and smacked him.

The only sound wood made when it hit flesh was a soft thud. Nothing like the movies, Victoria thought as the man crumpled to the ground.

"Jesus, lady," the lone man standing whispered.

She aimed the bat his way. "Stay put."

The man nodded his head and took one step back.

Bending to Gabriel, she ran her hand over his cheek, through his hair, to assess the damage. "Gabriel. Gabriel, wake up, darling."

His low moan said he was close to consciousness, but not quite there. She slapped his cheek. "Gabriel! Wake up!"

His hand floated up in an unsteady journey to his head. "Sweet baby Jesus," he groaned.

"Are you all right?" she asked breathlessly.

"Victoria?"

She helped him stand. His head swiveled from her face to the ground, to the bat still clutched in her hand. Twice. "You?"

She nodded. "I'm catching on to this covert cops-and-robbers stuff. Kind of exciting once you get used to it."

"Call the police," he said, staring at her.

"I did."

"She did," Gabe muttered to himself, unable to pull everything together. His aching, concussed head wasn't absorbing it all. "Where are the kids?"

"In the family room. I wouldn't let them come out."

He shook his head in wide-eyed amazement. "Thank God for small favors."

Within fifteen minutes, a sheriff's deputy had arrived. Within forty-five minutes, both intruders were en route to the Douglas County Correctional Facility. Within fifty minutes, Gabe had delivered a stern lecture to all four Devereauxs.

"No red lights," Michael commented. "That's not the way they did it on TV."

"Yeah, no sirens, either," Jill added glumly.

"This isn't a *Magnum* rerun!" Gabe roared. "Do you know how dangerous this was? Two armed men lurking around. My God, it was only a stroke of luck—" he glared at Victoria "—that we're all here now."

"Gabe," Anastasia said quietly.

"Not now, short stuff." He focused on Victoria. He could've lost her. Why the hell had she risked her life for his miserable hide? "Never, and I mean ever—"

"Gabe—" Anastasia interrupted.

"Not now, short stuff."

"But, Gabe!"

The child wasn't going to let it drop. He fell to one knee and took her shoulders between his palms. "What is it?"

Her gaze fell to the floor. Her big toe ground into the carpet. "Why'd those men hurt you?"

Grasping her chin between thumb and forefinger, he tilted her face up. "Remember your uncle's package, the one that disappeared?" She nodded. "That's what they wanted."

"Is it 'mportant?"

"Yeah, sugar, it sure is."

"Will you stay if I find it?"

Gabe's jaw slackened. He stared at the child. "You know where it is?"

Anastasia's jaw snapped to an angle inherited from her mother. Set and stubborn.

"Sweetheart," Victoria said. "If you know something, tell Gabriel. We can't barter for his love."

Her gaze caught his, meshed and mingled in a silent understatement. No, they didn't have to barter for his love; he'd given it freely once, but again? Did they really want it? It was too much to hope for—

"Molly's got it," Anastasia announced. "But there's not very much left. She chewed it all up, an' I didn't want Uncle Bruce to get mad at her and kick her again. I hate it when he's mean."

Over Anastasia's head, Gabe's gaze met Victoria's. Shock, disillusionment, disappointment, all warred for supremacy in her elegant face. "I'll check out Molly and the doghouse," he said. "And this time, stay here."

Victoria had resettled the children in their beds. After all the excitement and adrenaline letdown, they fell asleep almost instantly. She wandered the upstairs aimlessly.

I didn't want to love you . . . it just happened.

So he did love her. If he thought she was going to step aside and let him go with a wring of her hands, he was stark, raving nuts. This time would be different. This time she'd stand and fight for the man she loved.

She stood quietly in the center of the family room, hands clasped in front of her. Her chest rose and fell in a rhythm Gabe found hypnotically fascinating, but then, she'd always fascinated him. "Victoria—"

"Gabriel—" she said at the same time, then lapsed into her controlled silence. "Go ahead."

"I'm sorry to bring this into your life," he said. She stood silent. His fingers kept busy brushing the remnant of the manila envelope Molly and Anastasia had heisted away. If he didn't do something constructive, he'd reach for her, and he couldn't bear to have her pull away. Dear God, she was so loyal, so courageous, so lovely. How could he let her go again?

Yet how could he stay? She had to be repulsed by the ugliness he'd brought. The specter of the shadows beckoned, the one place he belonged, where he was comfortable. She'd flung open the gates of his self-imposed exile and touched his rusty heart with life and love. She'd reminded him of the goodness life had to offer, the softness that could be found in love's embrace. And how had he repaid her? By dragging her down into the dirt with him. She couldn't want him after that.

Still she said nothing, showing him how much emptier the silence would be without her, how much more miserable the loneliness. He wouldn't hurt her again. "I'm sorry," he said sincerely. "I wish I could've spared you all this."

"I don't want your apologies."

His head snapped up. "Then what do you want?"

"You."

He shook his head. "Victoria, you've had a helluva night. You're exhausted, and you aren't thinking clearly."

"Ridiculous. I'm thinking very clearly." She stepped forward, hips swaying under her satiny robe. "For example, I'm thinking you're remarkably brave—"

"Right," he scoffed. "That's why I manipulated you into leaving the house the day I nabbed your brother."

She took another step. "You're incredibly gener-
ous—"

"Sure," he drawled, wanting to soak in her words,
believe what he was hearing, but too afraid to grab on
to it for fear he'd screw up again. "That's why I strong-
armed my way in here in the first place."

"And kind—"

"I made love to you under false pretenses," he
growled. "How kind was that?"

"And strong—"

"Not strong enough to protect you and the kids. You
rescued me, remember?"

She took another slow step. "When are you going
to forgive yourself for living when your family died?"
she asked. "It isn't up to you to be invincible, just to
do the best you can. I don't want you to be superhu-
man, just yourself, with feet of clay."

Gabe teetered on a pinnacle: go on punishing himself
for being human, or be human and carry on as best he
could. A heartbeat passed before he pulled her to him.
"Run those sterling qualities of mine by me again,"
he said with the beginnings of a grin. "I need a re-
fresher course."

She slipped her arms around his waist and rubbed her
cheek against his bare chest. "You're also a wonderful
cook."

"Too true," he said.

"Tell me you love me again," she breathed.

"I love you again." He held her in the silence, unable to grasp the reality.

She heaved a hearty sigh and angled her head back
to look at him. "So kiss me, tough guy. I've already
done most of the work tonight."

His voice deepened, and his eyes darkened with increasing desire. "Oh, really?"

Her eyes sparkled as a smile touched her lips. "First I blurted out that I love you, then I rescued you, and—"

He kissed her leisurely, tasted her thoroughly, relished her softness pressed intimately against his hardness. "I love you, Mrs.-Devercaux-soon-to-be-Mrs.-Sanders," he said, and lowered his head to hers again. "More than I can ever say."

"Is that a proposal?" she whispered, and leaned into his kiss.

"Damn betcha, and you'd better not decline." He lifted her in his arms, cradling her close and took the stairs two at a time.

She looped her arms around his neck and nibbled on his earlobe. "I wouldn't think of it."

Inside her bedroom he kissed her with growing need, increasing heat, giving vent to the love and longing held back through too many dark years.

"Don't ever leave me again," she murmured. Her hands roamed over him, unsnapping, unzipping, maneuvering until he was as breathless as she.

"Never," he swore, and took her mouth in another searing kiss. "You wield a mean baseball bat."

"Yes. I do." She held him close, reveling in the shelter of his arms. He pressed her down on the bed, his hands seeking, searching, bringing delicious sensations. "Ah . . . Oh, Gabriel," she sighed.

"Call me Gabe," he breathed, and filled her body with his. Only with this woman did he feel the peace and contentment he'd sought. Only she could heal him. Only with her had he found his way back.

"Welcome home . . . Gabe."

EPILOGUE

"One, two, three-pant, blow, remember?" Gabe anxiously urged his wife.

Sweat trickled down Victoria's temples, her breath rasping in and out of her dry, open mouth. "Of course I remember," she snapped. "Who do you think was next to you through all those Lamaze classes, you idiot?"

Gabe grinned like a cheshire cat, thoroughly enjoying the sights and sounds of labor. "You're yelling at me. That's great! You're in transition. We're almost there."

"What's this 'we' stuff?" An invisible vise squeezed Victoria's swollen belly, and she groaned, but panted as per his instructions. Her husband of eight months was taking his job as Lamaze coach seriously, but she wouldn't deny him a moment. His perpetual frown and the pain she'd too often witnessed in his eyes in the past had all but disappeared. He'd turned out much as she'd known he would: constant, solid, a man to share her life with, and—to quote his matchless, arrogant description—one helluva lover. Which is how she'd gotten into her current state.

"Okay, babe," Gabe said, positioning himself behind her shoulders. "The doctor says we can push on the next one."

"Quit saying 'we'!" she groused, unable to help the snappish words directed at the man she loved more than life.

"*We* got into this together," he gently reminded her, "and *we* will get out of it together—just like *we* do everything else, my love."

Another fierce twist across her abdomen prevented any comeback from Victoria. Gabe grabbed her shoulders in his warm, solid hands. "Push," he whispered against her ear. "Push!"

They repeated the scene four more times before the green-clad obstetrician smiled at them. "Congratulations," she said, "You have a perfect baby girl."

"A girl?" Gabe watched the doctor place a thoughtful, but messy, wrinkled baby on his wife's belly. He blinked the mist out of his eyes. "A girl," he repeated reverently, and kissed Victoria's damp cheek.

"I take it that's okay?" Victoria asked with a weary smile as the nurse whisked the child to the other side of the room for cleanup and Apgar readings.

"It's more than okay," Gabe said, and captured Victoria's lips in a fierce kiss.

Once more a harsh contraction seized Victoria's belly, catching her off guard. She grabbed Gabriel's hand and squeezed hard. "Something's wrong," she whispered.

Panic knifed through Gabe. "What's going on?" he barked in his most commanding voice.

The obstetrician's soft blue eyes crinkled at the corners as if to say, *I've seen this all before.* "Get back to your post, coach," she said, obviously enjoying Gabe's discomposure. "We've got another baby to birth."

"Twins?" Gabe and Victoria looked at each other in disbelief. "But how? Why?"

"Push now!" the doctor ordered. "Talk later."

Gabe held his wife's shoulders once more, speechless and dumbfounded. Three strong pushes later, a sturdy son tumbled kicking and squalling into the world.

"That'll be one to watch," the doctor said, handing the child to the nurse. "He hid from me and my medical equipment for eight months. Slippery little devil, but it's not unusual. Every once in a while Mother Nature catches modern medicine off guard," she said. "Keeps us on our toes."

"A lot like his father," Victoria murmured with a smile.

Fifteen minutes later, Gabe held his daughter, while Victoria nursed their demanding son. "I still can't believe it. Are you upset about two?" he asked.

"Overwhelmed maybe, but never upset," Victoria said, with tear-spangled eyes. "We'll definitely need extra help around the house again."

"But this time you'll make sure the nanny's a real nanny," he sagely observed.

"Yeah." An impudent grin crept out. "Look where it got me this time."

Tucking the pink-bundled baby into the hospital bassinet, Gabe sighed. "I've got to report to the troops. They're probably tearing the waiting room end from end by now." He dropped a soft kiss on Victoria's waiting lips.

"Thank you, Gabe," she whispered. "I love you so."

"And I love you." His soft hazel gaze met and meshed with hers. "But when are you gonna get this thing right?" He smiled. "I'm the one that should be thanking you. And I will. For the rest of our lives."

SHARE THE FUN . . .
SHARE YOUR NEW-FOUND TREASURE!!

You don't want to let your new books out of your sight? That's okay. Your friends can get their own. Order below.

No. 123 LIES AND SHADOWS by Pam Hart
Gabe certainly did not fit Victoria's image of the perfect nanny!

No. 30 REMEMBER THE NIGHT by Sally Falcon
Joanna throws caution to the wind. Is Nathan fantasy or reality?

No. 31 WINGS OF LOVE by Linda Windsor
Mac & Kelly soar to new heights of ecstasy. Are they ready?

No. 32 SWEET LAND OF LIBERTY by Ellen Kelly
Brock has a secret and Liberty's freedom could be in serious jeopardy!

No. 33 A TOUCH OF LOVE by Patricia Hagan
Kelly seeks peace and quiet and finds paradise in Mike's arms.

No. 34 NO EASY TASK by Chloe Summers
Hunter is wary when Doone delivers a package that will change his life.

No. 35 DIAMOND ON ICE by Lacey Dancer
Diana could melt even the coldest of hearts. Jason hasn't a chance.

No. 36 DADDY'S GIRL by Janice Kaiser
Slade wants more than Andrea is willing to give. Who wins?

No. 37 ROSES by Caitlin Randall
It's an inside job & K.C. helps Brett find more than the thief!

No. 38 HEARTS COLLIDE by Ann Patrick
Matthew finds big trouble and it's spelled P-a-u-l-a.

No. 39 QUINN'S INHERITANCE by Judi Lind
Gabe and Quinn share an inheritance and find an even greater fortune.

No. 40 CATCH A RISING STAR by Laura Phillips
Justin is seeking fame; Beth helps him find something more important.

No. 41 SPIDER'S WEB by Allie Jordan
Silvia's quiet life explodes when Fletcher shows up on her doorstep.

No. 42 TRUE COLORS by Dixie DuBois
Julian helps Nikki find herself again but will she have room for him?

No. 43 DUET by Patricia Collinge
Adam & Marina fit together like two perfect parts of a puzzle!

No. 44 DEADLY COINCIDENCE by Denise Richards
J.D.'s instincts tell him he's not wrong; Laurie's heart says trust him.

No. 45 PERSONAL BEST by Margaret Watson
Nick is a cynic; Tess, an optimist. Where does love fit in?

No. 46 ONE ON ONE by JoAnn Barbour
Vincent's no saint but Loie's attracted to the devil in him anyway.

No. 47 STERLING'S REASONS by Joey Light
Joe is running from his conscience; Sterling helps him find peace.

No. 48 SNOW SOUNDS by Heather Williams
In the quiet of the mountain, Tanner and Melaine find each other again.

No. 49 SUNLIGHT ON SHADOWS by Lacey Dancer
Matt and Miranda bring out the sunlight in each other's lives.

No. 50 RENEGADE TEXAN by Becky Barker
Rane lives only for himself—that is, until he meets Tamara.

No. 51 RISKY BUSINESS by Jane Kidwell
Blair goes undercover but finds more than she bargained for with Logan.

No. 52 CAROLINA COMPROMISE by Nancy Knight
Richard falls for Dee and the glorious Old South. Can he have both?